W9-BCI-346

RULES TO
ROCK BY

RULES TO ROCK BY

JOSH FARRAR

Walker & Company ✳ New York

Copyright © 2010 by Josh Farrar
All rights reserved. No part of this book may be reproduced or transmitted in any
form or by any means, electronic or mechanical, including photocopying, recording,
or by any information storage and retrieval system, without permission in writing
from the publisher.

First published in the United States of America in July 2010 by
Walker Publishing Company, Inc., a division of Bloomsbury Publishing, Inc.
www.bloomsburyteens.com

For information about permission to reproduce selections from this book, write to
Permissions, Walker BFYR, 175 Fifth Avenue, New York, New York 10010

Library of Congress Cataloging-in-Publication Data
Farrar, Josh.
Rules to rock by / By Josh Farrar.
p.   cm.
Summary: Annabella Cabrera tries to start a rock band at her new middle school in
Providence, Rhode Island, but has trouble when the members of a rival band bully
her and she develops a case of writer's block.
ISBN 978-0-8027-2079-5
[1. Rock groups—Fiction. 2. Interpersonal relations—Fiction. 3. Middle schools—
Fiction. 4. Schools—Fiction. 5. Rhode Island—Fiction.] I. Title.
PZ7.F2432Ru 2010   [Fic]—dc22   2009040207

Book design by Danielle Delaney
Typeset by Westchester Book Composition
Printed in the U.S.A. by Quebecor World Fairfield, Pennsylvania
2 4 6 8 10 9 7 5 3 1

All papers used by Bloombury Publishing, Inc., are natural, recyclable products
made from wood grown in well-managed forests. The manufacturing processes
conform to the environmental regulations of the country of origin.

R0425995240

For Chris Daddio

RULES TO ROCK BY

ROCK 'N' ROLL HAS-BEEN

You'd never guess it now, but I used to be a rock star.

And I don't mean that my mom or dad gave me a high five and called me a "total rock star" after I won a spelling bee or something. I mean, I was a *real* rock star, the bassist of Egg Mountain, the most popular kid band in New York. We played to packed clubs all over the city, did interviews, and posed for local magazine spreads. Strangers approached us on the street, gushing praise. Sure, our fan base was mostly in Brooklyn and Manhattan, but I knew we were on the verge of making it big. How? Well, for one, we were starting to get e-mails from all over the country, even from overseas, from people who had heard us on the Internet. Also, people from record labels had started to sniff around, asking us what our plans for the future were. But mostly, I knew we were going to be rock stars when my favorite bass player and number one rock 'n' roll idol, Satomi Matsuzaki of Deerhoof, asked *me*, Annabelle Cabrera, for an autograph. I was living the dream.

But now, at age twelve, I was a has-been. I hadn't been on a stage in over three months. My dream was dead.

I was lying on my bed in a crazy-hot loft apartment in Providence, Rhode Island, trying to pretend that my nine-year-old brother's snoring wasn't about to make me scream like an insane person. Rhode Island! The whole state's about as big as a guitar pick, and I was stuck in it for good. So I lay there, sweating in the sticky summer heat, trying to comfort myself with my best memories. I put the fan on high, listened to the Egg Mountain playlist on my iPod, and tried to live the good parts all over again. You could say I was trying to press the rewind button on my entire life.

Like the time I strapped on Satomi, my trusty 1978 Ibanez Roadster—the beat-up but reliable bass guitar given to me by my dad on my eighth birthday and which I'd immediately named after Satomi Matsuzaki—and prepared to walk onto Central Park SummerStage with the other members of Egg Mountain. Ronaldo on vocals and rhythm guitar. Dakota on drums. Fast Eddie Amatruda playing lead. We were opening for Deerhoof, one of the only worthwhile bands left on the planet. The *real* Satomi would be looking on, and three thousand people were in the audience, waiting to see if we could pull off our most high-profile gig ever.

I'll admit it. I was freaking out. I was supposed to sing lead on the first song, "Climbing the Egg," and I could barely breathe. I felt like somebody had sewn my throat shut.

Ronaldo stood behind the drum kit and called us over. These were our last moments together before we would face our biggest audience ever. We stood in a circle and put our hands together, like a football team before *hut-hut-hike*. I made sure my hand didn't quite touch the others—my palms were sweating like crazy. I leaned on Fast Eddie, not out of camaraderie but because I thought I was about to pass out.

"This is it, you guys," said Ronaldo. "Everything we've been working on for a year comes down to the next thirty-five minutes. This is the biggest stage we've ever played. Don't forget this night. Make it count."

"Yeah!" Eddie and Dakota cried while I lip-synched.

We raised our arms in unison, and I looked straight up, catching a view of the darkening sky. Then, as we walked onstage, I couldn't take my eyes off the nightscape above us. I gazed up at a million stars just starting to appear and felt so tiny. Then the spotlights came on and hit me right in the face. I was blinded, absolutely frozen.

"Annabelle," Ronaldo whispered. "You okay?"

I used my hand for a visor and looked for family and friends in the crowd. But all I could see was white light pounding into my brain.

"Earth to Annabelle Cabrera?" Ronaldo said. "Come on, you can do this. It's just like any other gig." He put his hands on my shoulders and gave them a quick squeeze, tilting his head down to meet my eyes. "You cool?"

"Yeah, I'm good," I said.

And I was. Just like that, I was fine. The crowd didn't matter; the lights didn't matter. Not even having my rock 'n' roll idol six feet away and scrutinizing my every move mattered. Only the music did. Only Egg Mountain. I looked down at Satomi and let my hand glide along her shiny frets. Then I checked my effects pedals, tapping them one by one with my right toe. Each time, a satisfying click resonated through the sole of my Chuck Taylor low-top. I breathed deeply once, then twice. I was ready.

Ronaldo went to his mic, coolly fired off the count, and nodded to me. I stepped up to my mic and sang the first two verses. I barely recognized my voice coming through the huge PA speakers, but when I looked out into the crowd, people were way into it, their heads bouncing up and down in time. Then Ronaldo joined me to scream out the chorus.

I'm climbin' the egg
I'm fightin' a nasty case of nerves
I'm hikin' my way along the white curve
I'm climbin' the egg
On my way to you

Dakota twirled his sticks in the air, landing with a thud on the downbeat. Fast Eddie's blistering guitar leads soared above us. I looked into the crowd. Kids pounded their fists on the stage and moshed in the pit. Adults' heads snapped back and forth as they played air guitar like teen metalheads. The audience sang along to every word.

I looked at Ronaldo. All we could do was throw our heads back and laugh. It was easily the greatest moment of my life so far. I was a rock star. And I was still two months shy of my twelfth birthday.

Okay, so maybe "rock star" is pushing it a little. *Budding* rock star? A bassist with a decent voice who happened to join a band at the moment they were about to explode?

Whatever. But before my parents decided to drag me to this ridiculous city, 180 miles away from my band, my grandmother, and everything I'd ever loved, I couldn't have imagined a better life. And I had no idea how hard it would be, how much I'd have to go through, to get it all back.

BAND FORMATION PLAN

Four months after the SummerStage concert, I stood on my tiptoes and scanned the pack of kids flooding through the halls, trying to find my new bandmates. It was my first day at Federal Hill Middle School, in Providence. I knew no one, and no one knew or noticed me. But that was only natural. I didn't expect a welcoming committee to run up and shower me with confetti and kisses. This was middle school, and I was new. I remembered a kid from my old school, D'Shawn Williams, who had been new in fifth grade. Nobody had talked to him—I mean, not a word—for the first six weeks of school, but by the end of the year he was one of the most popular kids in our class. So I expected to be ignored at first and told myself it wouldn't last long. Or so I thought.

I hooked my thumbs under the straps of the gig bag—

basically a backpack specially made for a bass, an accessory that screams *band camp!* to some but *rocker!* to people who know better—which held Satomi and followed the signs to the registrar's office.

"Annabelle Cabrera," I said to a little bald man sitting behind a desk. "Sixth grade."

"You'd better hurry," he said. He crinkled his nose, like there was a bad smell in the air. "Your math class starts in three minutes."

"Where's my homeroom?"

"Sixth graders don't have homerooms. You need to get to room 17. Better run."

I didn't run. I didn't want to be out of breath.

Rock stars are never out of breath.

I wasn't the only one still in the hall. Everyone at Federal Hill was juicing the last three minutes of summer. Two gum-snapping, flat-ironed girls stood chatting in front of the activities board. Tight-fitting tank tops, acid-wash denim skirts. I knew girls like this back in Brooklyn. Plenty of them. They spent more time on hair than homework. Their brains were not the part of their bodies they wanted to develop. They had to be eighth graders, dressed like that.

"Fool said what?" one said. "Unbelievable."

The girls turned their heads as a bunch of boys raced down the hall, pushing people over without even noticing. Seventh graders, probably. Big, and not too bright. I tried to write song lyrics about them in my head, but I couldn't come up with anything but a title: "Dumb Puppies."

Or something like that. I had just started writing songs,

and I wasn't great at it yet. In the meantime I just wanted these guys to pass me by without pushing me over. I didn't want to get knocked down, especially on my first day.

The flat-ironed girls ignored the dumb-puppy show. They rolled their eyes like annoyed older sisters and went back to what they were talking about. Who wants a dumb puppy for a boyfriend anyway? Maybe they were smarter than they seemed.

My first few looks at Federal Hill had been disappointing. I had thought Providence would be different from Brooklyn. It's a small town, but it has a big college and a wacky art school. I figured there'd be lots of kids into weird movies and excellent music. But where were they? I was surrounded by Latin American princesses and wannabe reggaeton thugs, just like at home. Where were all the rockers?

☆

After math, on my way to the art room, I noticed a big, burly dude leaning against a locker. He wore a rock band T-shirt, and a long wallet chain hung from his belt loop, dangling against black jeans. Definitely a rocker.

I started to talk myself through what to do: *Just walk right up to him and calmly tell him that you're starting a band.* It sounded easy enough. But I wasn't ready, I guess, so I hung back and checked him out. The guy was huge and mean-looking, with loads of dark curly hair. He was wearing a Mastodon T-shirt. I knew Mastodon and they weren't really my thing—too metal, too crazy, just too much. The shirt showed Bigfoot feasting on a helpless deer. Lovely.

I watched as Curly Burly pushed a kid up against a locker. Then CB riffled through the little guy's sweatshirt pocket and pulled out a wad of cash. The kid was blond and so tiny he looked like a fifth grader who had skipped half the grades in elementary school. He was quiet as the bully took his cash, not resisting one bit—this was definitely a scene that had taken place many times before. Maybe every day.

Then Curly Burly turned to leave, but stopped right in front of me and smirked. Perfect.

"The Beatles, huh?" he said, nodding at my hoodie. "Lame."

"No, they're not," I said before my brain could kick in.

"What did you say to me, girl?"

"The Beatles are not lame," I said, crossing my arms.

If he wanted an excuse to turn me into mush, I had just handed it to him.

But he just laughed. "In the future, no eye contact," he said, purposely brushing my shoulder as he passed me, knocking me a couple inches back on my heels. "Got it?"

I tried not to think about Curly Burly as he walked away. So there was an unwritten rule that little kids had to give him their cash and nobody was allowed to look him in the eye. Big deal. It was stupid to have talked back to him, but I had done it and, hopefully, had gotten away with it. I might have just painted a future target sign on my own back, but I didn't care. I wasn't at Federal Hill to make friends. I was there to put together my band. So Curly Burly could go about his business, and I'd go about mine.

Rock stars don't scare that *easy.*

☆

I mostly daydreamed my way through art. It didn't matter—nothing happens on the first day of school. It's just introductions and hopeful teacher talk. By the third week, they usually don't sound so hopeful anymore.

I tried to come up with a band formation plan. Should I post a sign? Walk up to any kid with a rock band T-shirt and tell him I wanted to take over the world with my music? The incident with Curly Burly had shown me that was not the way to go. Some people with rock band T-shirts are not that friendly.

How could I make myself known in Providence without coming on too strong? How could I appear incredibly cool without trying too hard? I was less than five feet tall and weighed eighty-eight pounds. I was beyond invisible. How could I get noticed?

I imagined myself standing on a table at lunchtime with Satomi and a massive 100-watt amp, cranking out heavy riffs while announcing in song that I was forming a band. Oh my God, I would get laughed out of the building! Terminated. Slaughtered.

I pulled out my notebook and wrote:

BAND FORMATION PLAN
by Annabelle Cabrera

1. Get the lay of the land. Observe. See how things work here. Don't stare at people too obviously. Hopefully don't get beaten up or made fun of.
2. Meet people. Musician people. Rockers.
3. Casually, coolly, tell them that I am starting a band.

4. Let the rockin' begin: club dates,
    recordings, interviews, photo shoots,
    videos, fame, etc.

☆

English class. One more period before lunch. Forty-five minutes before I could see how things really worked at Federal Hill. I was getting fidgety, so I practiced secret bass scales under my desk while a short, dark man with tortoiseshell glasses introduced himself.

"I am Mr. Venketaswami, and I will be instructing you in English this year," he said in a slow, melodic Indian accent. He wore a wine red button-down shirt with a very small collar and a navy crewneck sweater. "Don't worry, you will not be tested on the spelling and pronunciation of my surname. You may call me Mr. V."

He waited for laughter. None came.

"Today we will start off with a bit of state-imposed activity." Mr. V smiled peacefully. "I will be assessing your reading fluency by having you read some charming passages aloud. You will be reading one at a time, so please entertain yourselves—silently—while you wait your turn."

Groans from the three kids who were actually listening.

I couldn't figure Mr. V out. His actual words were super serious, but his eyes sparkled while he spoke them. He seemed to be laughing inside, as if the test were a secret joke he was sharing with us. Walking slowly and deliberately through the rows of desks, he carried a roster in his left hand and a tiny chair, which could have belonged to a first grader, in his right. He spent less than three minutes with each kid, quietly making his way around the classroom in alphabetical order. "I should have had you sit in neat rows, from A to Z," he said. "Oh well, at least I am getting my exercise."

It didn't take him long to reach the C's. "Annabelle Cabrera?" Mr. V asked gently, sliding his baby chair alongside me. Unbelievably, he seemed to fit in it quite comfortably. The man's hips must have been slimmer than mine. And I have no hips.

"Yep."

"I hope you might enjoy this little assessment. I know I will enjoy hearing the passages for the fourth time in the last five minutes." He smirked, and I smiled back. He was *definitely* making fun of this test. I grabbed the sheet of paper he handed me. "Just read aloud in your natural voice, easy as pie," he said. "Easy as pie. What an odd phrase this is. What is so easy about pie? It is very *difficult* to make a pie. Difficult, indeed . . . please excuse me, Ms. Cabrera. My mind wanders. Let's begin with the passages."

There wasn't much to read, just a couple short paragraphs. It didn't look hard. I started:

Many people use the expression "Money makes the world go 'round." While money does not physically make Earth rotate around the sun, money is an important tool that human beings use to exchange goods and services.

Who had written this thing? Money doesn't physically make Earth rotate around the sun? Oh boy. Were there random lonely people cranking out these reading passages in a basement somewhere while the rest of the world went about its business?

"Aren't we a little old for this?" I asked.

"According to the Rhode Island Department of Education, no school-age child is too old for a bit of nonsensical and irrelevant reading material." He smiled and raised his left eyebrow slightly. "Please continue. I assure you it is quite painless."

At the grocery store, people spend money to pay for goods such as milk, vegetables, and meat. Also, the people who own the grocery store use money to pay the farmers who supply these goods. The farmers and the grocers get paid with money, and you get to eat!

Sure, the farmers and the grocers get paid. But who gets paid to write this junk?

"Okay," I said. "That was . . . stimulating."

"It is not meant to be stimulating, Ms. Cabrera, only readable," said Mr. V. And in a whisper: "And you should be glad to know that you are reading at a sixth-grade level. Congratulations."

"I'm *in* sixth grade."

"Very few Federal Hill sixth graders read on grade level, Ms. Cabrera," he whispered.

When the bell rang—lunch, finally!—I was out of my seat in a nanosecond.

"Take it easy, Ms. Cabrera," Mr. V said with a playful smirk. "Slow and steady wins the race."

Yeah, right. How could I stay slow and steady when my future band members were somewhere out in those halls? I jogged toward the cafeteria, but made sure to slow down before I got there.

Rock stars don't jog. They strut.

☆

In Sunset Park, Brooklyn, at PS 443, almost every kid in my school had been into hip-hop and reggaeton. The kids who even knew who The Beatles were thought they were just some pasty old English guys whose music didn't matter anymore. They all thought I was a total freak for being so into old music. Except Ronaldo.

Ronaldo Duffy was two years older than me. Like me, he also had one Latin parent and one white one—his mom was Puerto Rican and his dad was Irish. And, also like me, he was a retro freak, except he thought it wasn't cool enough to just like The Beatles. "Everybody likes them," he would say. "But have you ever heard The Kinks? The Troggs? The Zombies?"

Ronaldo had *style.* The dude really knew how to dress. Plus, I gave him bonus points for pulling it off in Sunset Park. PS 443 was no fancy private school. You could get beaten *down* for looking different, but Ronaldo didn't care. All the other boys, even the very poorest ones in a neighborhood where sharing your bedroom with only *one* brother or sister made you the equivalent of Hilton-rich, had to wear the best brands. Even if it meant wearing the same two outfits over and over again. These guys would strut around, all puffed out, swiveling their chests in every girl's direction so nobody could miss the label. And by fifth grade, some kids were even starting to sport chains. Fake gold, but still.

Ronaldo got his style off the backs of his dad's punk album covers, stealing all those ideas and then mixing in his own until he looked like a cross between Edward Scissorhands and the bassist from The Clash. He angled an old-school white-rimmed Cuban hat on his head, saying, "That Clash guy stole his look from Spanish dudes—I'm just stealing it back." He wore his jeans so tight it looked like he had to steam them off, then tied a bandanna around one ankle. He laughed it off when the thug wannabes pushed him into the lockers or followed him onto the street, calling him *pendejo*. Ronaldo was willing to take a beating every once in a while; he was going to keep dressing the way he pleased, to keep being who he wanted to be, and none of the B-boys could stop him.

One day at the beginning of fifth grade—just like Federal Hill, PS 443 had been a fifth-through-eighth middle school—Ronaldo approached me in the hall. I already knew who he was, of course, and I thought he was the coolest thing ever. I was so surprised, I actually looked behind me, once over each shoulder, before realizing he wanted to talk to *me*. Egg Mountain, who had already been gigging around town at all-ages clubs, had lost their bassist. He had heard I played, and he wanted to give me a try.

It didn't take more than one practice for Ronaldo to see that I knew my way around the bass. I was in the band before I even knew what hit me.

Ronaldo was an amazing leader. He had stage presence, great taste, and a plan of action from the very beginning. He helped the rest of us pick clothes that looked cool on us and made us look like a real band when we were onstage. He had picked the name Egg Mountain a few months earlier, saying he had heard it in a dream. "I don't care if the name sounds weird," he said. "People will remember it." And they did. By the time I joined, Egg Mountain had already landed gigs at kid-band afternoons in clubs in Brooklyn and Manhattan. A month later, we were opening up for Blitzen Trapper at the Mercury Lounge and headlining our own shows at Pete's Candy Store, where we packed the house.

By summertime, we were one of the biggest local acts in the city, kid *or* adult, and because I was the lead singer of three songs, the bassist, and the only girl in the band, I had tons of fans. But more importantly, I had found somewhere I belonged. My favorite times in the band actually weren't even in public. I loved practicing and, even more, hanging out during and after practice. Fast Eddie was hilarious and told the most amazing jokes. He and Ronaldo played off each other like pint-sized kings of comedy, and their routine always had Dakota and me doubled over in spastic laughing fits.

Nobody in the band ever seemed to care about my gender. I wasn't a girl to them; I was a *bandmate.* And being a bandmate was the only place outside of my family where I felt like I mattered, where I felt like I belonged. Unlike in school, I could say whatever I wanted and not worry about what people would think. Those three guys took me seriously and cared about what I had to say, from day one. So it wasn't the roar of the crowd that I missed the most—although I'd be lying if I said I didn't love that, too—so much as just *being in the band.* I missed that feeling, that incredible sensation of being a part of something bigger than myself, and I wanted it back.

Rock stars don't like to be alone.

☆

Lunch at Federal Hill looked pretty much like lunch at my old school: cardboard burgers, pasty potatoes, an overcooked mystery vegetable. And that wasn't the only thing that reminded me of school in Brooklyn. Without even trying, I had somehow landed in Loner Land. At least that's what they would have called this table of loser outcasts at PS 443. I wasn't looking for friends, it's true. But I had never been pushed *this* far to the sidelines in Brooklyn. For the first time, I was seeing Loner Land from the inside out.

To my left sat a freckly boy whose index finger seemed to be permanently wedged up his nose. How could he eat his plasticized burger with that finger in the way? Somehow he managed. To my right, a tiny, eyelinered girl dressed head to toe in black, an evil kitty logo on her T-shirt, read aloud from a book perched on her lap. It was *David Copperfield.* She whispered the dialogue in a foppy British accent.

I had seen these kids before. Every school had them. Federal Hill might have had new players, but it was the same old game.

I looked back at the *David Copperfield* girl, searching for hidden promise. Goths were always super into whatever they were doing. Like me, they were obsessed. The key was, what were they obsessed with? This one might have been adapting the eight-hundred-page book she was reading into a seriously strange rock opera. Or she might have been plotting ways to murder the family cat. With goths, you never knew.

I took a deep breath and approached her.

"How's it going?" I asked.

"Are you addressing me?" I could tell it was a mistake right away. The girl didn't drop the British accent, even when not reciting from her book.

"Um . . . yep."

"Forgive me, but I'm in the middle of an especially propulsive chapter. I'd like to continue reading."

I stared at her for a second. My mouth was probably hanging half open.

"It's Dickens!" Goth Girl cried. "I'm in the middle of a cliffhanger!"

"Okay, whatever. Enjoy your reading, I guess."

I looked around the massive room. Two tables of cave-dwelling hip-hop thugs; a mixed-gender nerd group in which kids appeared to be quizzing each other from a pre-algebra textbook; one wannabe-exclusive table of giggling, pink-nail-polished glamour girls. And the all-important miscellaneous extreme-loser table—well, I was sitting at it.

I tried to reassure myself with the thought that if Ronaldo had formed Egg Mountain from the ruins of PS 443, I should be able to pull off the same thing at this dump.

"So you're into The Beatles?" a raspy-voiced girl asked, nodding at my hoodie, which, I realized, was responsible for pretty much every social interaction I had had that day.

"Yeah. You?"

"Totally. George is the best. I like 'Here Comes the Sun.'"

This girl was wack. She knew who had written "Here Comes the Sun," which was promising. But she confused me. She had such a deep, scratchy voice, but she was pretty, blond, and very put-together. Her white jeans were spotless. My old school didn't have kids like this; in Brooklyn, this girl would have been private school all the way. Still, though, even if I was paying attention to her for the wrong reasons, she was into The Beatles! It was worth a shot.

"So, hey, I'm a musician, and I'm trying to start a band. Do you know any musicians around here I could talk to?"

"Well, there's this band Raising Cain. But you don't want to talk to them. Those guys are animals."

"Okay . . ." Another band? Maybe I was being naive, but I had sort of hoped I'd have the only band at Federal Hill. Egg Mountain had been the only band at PS 443. Still, Raising Cain probably wasn't any good, even if their name did sound kind of cool.

"I'm a musician, though." The girl sounded like she had a cold, or cake crumbs lodged in her throat.

"Yeah? What do you play?"

"I sing."

And right then and there, she busted out into song, smack-dab in the middle of the cafeteria. I could immediately see how, despite her prettiness and girly-girl style, this spaz was stranded in Loner Land.

"And the earth, it was a poem," she sang. "And the poem made me cry. And maybe die inside, just a little . . ."

Oh no, I thought. *Musical theater!*

The girl's singing voice was froglike, too. She coughed a couple of times, but she still sounded like a chain-smoking sixty-two-year-old. On top of that, she couldn't keep still. She kept clicking a ballpoint pen in her hand, and she walked around in circles while she sang. As the song started to build, she circled faster and faster, moving toward the center of the cafeteria. She seemed close to a literally dizzying climax. Kids with lunch trays had to swerve out of the way to avoid her. She looked like a nut.

I glanced down at my notebook, hoping the entire cafeteria wasn't looking over at us yet. *See how things work here,* my Band Formation Plan said. *Hopefully don't get beaten up or made fun of.* Five minutes of this and I would be more than teased—in people's minds I'd be connected with this crazy girl for the next year.

"Then the eagles flew to me, and in their cries I heard a wisdom," she sang. "And they kept my love alive."

Speaking of eagles, a few kids started to point, as if they had just spotted a rare form of wildlife right here at Federal Hill. The "audition" was obviously about as done as the lifeless burgers on our plates. It was damage-control time now. I had to get this drama queen out of the caff before this became the most talked-about incident of the first month of school.

"Hey, could we maybe do this somewhere quieter?" I tried to interrupt. But she was so wrapped up in what she was doing, she couldn't even hear me. Meanwhile, about eight boys had gathered around us, pointing and laughing, while this nut continued to sing her god-awful lyrics. Three of them even started to dance in a circle around us, pretending to be inspired by the cheesy soundtrack she sang out.

Finally, the girl realized what was happening. And she

totally snapped. "Oh my God, will no one ever understand me at this school?" she said, her lower lip shaking in anger. I had to keep myself from looking around for video cameras, because these tantrum antics couldn't have been real; there had to be a live studio audience somewhere. "Am I not even good enough to make a new girl's stupid band? Ridiculous!" She turned abruptly and walked away.

"Umm, nice to meet you!" I called out after her. What a weirdo.

I opened the door to the hall. A couple of kids pointed and chuckled. "Nice song," one said.

I was totally embarrassed, but I tried not to show it.

Rock stars don't blush.

A Homecoming, Sort of

I turned my key in the lock.

"Hey, guys, I'm home!" I called out.

No answer.

"From my first day of school. In a new city!"

Still nothing.

"I got home fine on the bus . . ."

My parents were definitely in here somewhere—I could smell half-burnt popcorn. They probably had headphones on.

I closed the door and looked out at the "studio," which was basically the entire center of our huge, messy loft apartment. My parents had moved us here so they could record and live on the cheap, and I had to hand it to them—they were doing what they said they would. My brother, Xavier, and I were miserable about our new hometown, but my parents' album was almost done.

Yep, there was my mom in the isolation booth, eyes closed and concentrating on recording a vocal part. I looked to the right, where my dad squinted at the computer in a makeshift control room. Dad was always the engineer, twiddling knobs and squinting into a computer monitor. I didn't see Xavier anywhere. Maybe Shaky Jake, my parents' drummer, was picking him up at school.

"Well, don't all come rushing to welcome me home. I'll just make myself a little snack." Still, no response.

I walked across the studio floor, and my mom finally noticed me. She gave me a wave and a smile but kept on singing. My dad gave me a thumbs-up sign without turning in my direction.

In the kitchen, I stood on my tiptoes to grab a package of wasabi rice crackers from the top of the fridge. Then I poured myself a big glass of grapefruit juice, grabbed the laptop we all shared, and headed to my "room," which was nothing more than a little square in the far left corner of the apartment, separated from my brother's "room" by a couple of flimsy Japanese screens. I'd be stretching it if I described this wimpy collection of screens as a "wall," too. They didn't reach more than halfway to the ceiling, so at night I could hear Xavier's every move. If his little nine-year-old body tossed and turned, I knew it. The soundtrack of my dreams was written by a snoring fourth grader.

I stepped into my *personal area*, bit into a rice cracker, and hit the space bar on the laptop. I figured I'd see if Ronaldo was on IM. He wasn't. But when I went to check out Egg Mountain's MySpace page for the three hundredth time in the last forty-eight hours, I saw the pleasing glow of the orange and green "online now" sign, and my heart leapt. I hadn't talked to Ronaldo in almost three days.

"Dude, get on IM. Hurry!!!!!" I typed in a MySpace message. I scanned the page. The band had 105,691 friends now, and "Climbing the Egg" had been played 597 times that day alone!

I scrolled down to check out the posts.

"Thanks for the add!" read one from SckBoy. "GOOD GOOD GOOD!!! Besos desde Buenos Aires!"

"Go crazy kids!!!" read a note from Mizayaki1121 in Japan.

"You rock! Hope to see you soon in France!" said Jolie-Ridicule.

Argentina, France, and Japan. Egg Mountain could launch an international tour whenever it wanted. With a total dork named Anthony Delaney playing my bass parts. Fantastic. I kept scrolling.

"New bassist looks like a good fit," said LightningBoltBoy. "But where's Annabelle?"

On the other end of the world, I wanted to answer. All alone. Just lonesome little Annabelle and Satomi, the loyal bass who is her only companion. I pictured the two of us thumbing a ride on the side of the highway, trying to hitchhike our way to rock 'n' roll stardom. Or at least away from obscurity and invisibility and toward . . . I don't know, if not Brooklyn, then at least somewhere where somebody knew my name.

"It's okay, Satomi. We'll get back in the game," I said, picking her up and plucking out the intro to "Climbing the Egg." I stood up and made some rock star poses in the full-length mirror in the corner of my room. This was something I did more often than I ever would have admitted, but how else could I know how other people saw me? And as long as I didn't get busted (X had caught me a couple times, but that doesn't count), it was fun.

I played "The Perfect Me" by Deerhoof and stared at my own reflection. Did I look like somebody who should be onstage? I pointed the neck of the bass up toward the ceiling and snarled. Thick, dark brown hair like my dad's, blue eyes like my mom's, but nothing special, nothing *different* about my face. I balanced the bass's body on my hip and stuck out my tongue. I wore rocker clothes: skinny jeans, a black-and-white checkered T-shirt, and my cherry red Converses. But there was nothing especially rock 'n' roll about *me*. I definitely didn't look as cool as either of my parents. My dad looked like a rock musician from the moment he woke up bleary-eyed till the moment he put his head on the pillow. And my mom was so pretty, with her black turtlenecks and dirty blond bangs. I was still only four foot ten! That officially made me a midget, not the offspring of indie-rock royalty. I would have to make up for it with attitude. I shook my hair out and tried a punky sneer. Did I look ridiculous? Maybe.

My laptop beeped. Ronaldo!

EggMtnRckr: Wassup belle?!?
Bassinyrface: nuuuuthin.
EggMtnRckr: total boredom?
Bassinyrface: First day of school. Blah . . .
EggMtnRckr: Heh, tell me about it. you got a new band yet?
Bassinyrface: It's only been 1 day, R.
EggMtnRckr: they dont know how to rawk in Pvidence?
Bassinyrface: ?

EggMtnRckr: I'm jk. see Liars on TV last night? Insane.

Bassinyrface: you know i'm not that into them.

EggMtnRckr: they are genius.

Bassinyrface: meh

EggMtnRckr: How bout yr parents. Album done?

Bassinyrface: nope. Endless.

EggMtnRckr: btw, what kind of mic does yr dad use for yr mom's vocals?

Bassinyrface: i dont know! stop kissing his butt all the time.

EggMtnRckr: i'm not kissing his butt!

Bassinyrface: meh.

EggMtnRckr: but the man IS genius. ☺

Bassinyrface: you go visit my grandmother like you said?

EggMtnRckr: Of course I saw Abuela! Got me some home cooking.

Bassinyrface: how's she seem?

EggMtnRckr: good.

Bassinyrface: details please?

EggMtnRckr: good, I dunno. Sad. She just kind of sat around.

Bassinyrface: she ask about me and X?

EggMtnRckr: on and on about you and X, yeah. Hey, Belle, sorry but I gotta go.

Bassinyrface: ok.

EggMtnRckr: Shooting video for Climbing . . .

Bassinyrface: ok, good luck. but it wont be the same without me!

EggMtnRckr: too true. but be happy for us, ok? we'll both

have bands soon, and we'll tour the world as a double bill. Cool?

Bassinyrface: yup.

EggMtnRckr: And next time, lets talk about YOUR band.

Bassinyrface: But I dont HAVE a band.

EggMtnRckr: Not yet. But you will soon. If you follow the rules.

Bassinyrface: rules?

EggMtnRckr: yeah, the Rules to Rock By.

Bassinyrface: umm, WHAT rules to rock by?

EggMtnRckr: mine, that's what. More later, Belle. Talk soon!

Bassinyrface: Ok, talk soon. Satomi says rock out on yr video, dude.

EggMtnRckr: Byeeeee!!!!!

Be happy for us. I made a promise to myself to try, but it felt horrible to be left out. I tried to remind myself that it wasn't Ronaldo's fault that my parents had pulled me out of Brooklyn. I was glad I was still in touch with Ronaldo—I think I would have gone crazy if I had landed in Providence and not been able to chat with him. He was like my lifeline to Brooklyn, to my grandmother, to my now former band. But I was amazed at how easily he seemed to be moving on since I had moved away. I mean, of course I was happy for him for shooting his stupid video! But I was supposed to be *in* the video. So did he expect me to do a cartwheel over the fact that Anthony Delaney was in it instead? I could be happy for Ronaldo, and Eddie and Dakota, too. But I couldn't help feeling sorry for myself, and I couldn't help secretly hoping that Anthony would fall on his face, forcing Ronaldo to beg me to take the Greyhound bus down to Port Authority to save them. He'd pick me up in a black Town Car, and we'd race to a top secret studio to shoot the video, where a pouting but relieved director would thank God that I had come down and rescued them all.

Now that that little daydream was over, I strapped Satomi back on, headed back to the kitchen, and ran straight into Shaky Jake, the big, broad-shouldered drummer who had been playing in my parents' band, Benny and Joon, for over ten years. Jake didn't officially live with us, but he spent a lot of nights on the couch.

"Oops, sorry, kiddo, close call," he said, rearing back to avoid getting clipped by Satomi's headstock. Jake was carrying more percussion instruments than he could comfortably handle, and his mop of red hair was pasted to his sweaty forehead. He had a set of bongos wedged between a rib and an arm, and a tambourine was wrapped around his wrist like a giant bracelet.

"I didn't even hear you come in. You pick up X?" I said.

"Yeah, he's with your mom in the booth." He dropped the tambourine.

"Looks like you've got your hands full, Jake."

"Yeah, can you help me out here?"

I picked up the tambourine and grabbed a shaker.

"Your mom's recording some vocals in there."

"I know."

"Wanna watch?"

"Meh." I followed him anyway, though. "She on take thirty-seven yet?"

"Nah, nah. Smooth as silk. She's only got one song to go, then *finito*. This magnum opus will be D-O-N-E."

My parents have been making albums since before I was born, so it isn't exactly a new experience for me to watch them record. But they had never recorded at home before. For my dad, who idolizes producers of records even more than the people who play on them, it was a dream come true. He had spent years trying to find a live/work space somewhere in New York, but he said it had gotten too expensive there. So he moved his whole family from the most happening city on the planet to the smallest state in the union, just so he could work on his records 24/7.

Jake gave me the *shh!* sign as we plopped down on the couch that divided the kitchen from the main part of the studio, and I tried to get myself into an educational frame of mind. Sure, it was a little much having my parents' band completely take over my life, but I had always learned a lot from watching them. When the time came for me to make *my* first real record—I wasn't counting Egg Mountain MP3s— I'd be way ahead of the game. Plus, it was a lot better than reciting reading passages for Mr. V.

X sat next to my mom in the vocal booth, a tiny room within a room that my dad and Jake had built for recording vocals and guitars. It looked like an actual room, only for a family of pixies. It was a pretty cozy spot, although my mom didn't look too cozy right then. Between tending to X, who was staying quiet at least for the time being, and recording probably her umpteenth take of whatever song they were singing, she looked like she couldn't wait to get out.

"Hon, I thought that last take was fine," she said through the microphone.

"It was, it was, babe," said my dad. "But we want better than 'fine,' right? We want . . . magic."

"Okay, okay." She smiled, but it looked like an effort. It was four fifteen p.m. I was trying to figure out how long this session had been going. They had been hard at it when Jake drove X and me to school that morning. Had they *started* in the morning, or was this an all-nighter about to hit its twenty-fourth hour? Still, Mom looked pretty. Even tired and zonked out, she looked fashion-modelly. I couldn't understand how she could look that good, even on zero sleep. I also couldn't understand how she could put up with my dad. He was seriously obsessing.

"All right, here we go," he said. "Take sixteen. Ready, and rolling . . ."

Shaky Jake twisted his fingers nervously through his orange beard.

My mom started singing again. Watching her, I remembered how hard she had tried to convince me that moving to Providence would be good for me, too. "It'll be a new start, Annabelle," she'd said. "You'll find a new band, and it'll be just as good as Egg Mountain. Better." I wasn't so sure about that, but at least my mom knew how good Egg Mountain was in the first place. Unlike my dad, she came to every gig that didn't conflict with Benny and Joon's schedule, and she supported me all the way.

She finished singing, and to my ears she sounded great. She didn't have a big voice—she couldn't hit loads of high notes like some singers on the radio—but it was calm and cool, with a little tease in it. I thought the take was great.

"Nice," my dad said, although I could tell that wasn't what he meant at all. "Very nice . . . but let's try it one more time."

"Aww, hon. Come on . . ." Mom looked like she was about to cry.

Jake caught my eye and nodded toward the door. X picked up on it, too, and slipped out of the booth to join us. We crept out as quickly and quietly as we had come in.

"Belle!" X cried out. "Rescue me! This is *sooo* boring."

"Okay, buddy, in a sec." X had never wanted to hang out this much in Brooklyn, but he was so starved for company in Providence that he was constantly hanging on me. It was half cute, half crazy-making.

"Sorry, guys," Jake said. "It was about to get a little tense in there."

"It already *was* a little tense in there," I said.

"Good point."

It wasn't the first time I had witnessed that scene this week. How could my dad, a guy who barely kept himself in clean socks, who would wear the same grimy T-shirt three days in a row, be such a perfectionist when it came to recording? How could he get on my mom's case about these tiny details, especially when just about every take she sang sounded perfect?

"Your dad always gets more . . . particular toward the end of a record," Jake said.

Don't get me wrong. I loved Benny and Joon. Or at least, I used to. They were the reason I wanted to start playing music.

And I had picked the bass—an instrument my parents usually did without—with the hopes of joining the group someday. I feel cheesy saying that now. Who wants to play music with their parents? But until I joined Egg Mountain, I had always dreamed that I would one day be *in* Benny and Joon, and that we could tour and record together. As a family.

That was a long time ago, though. Now being in Benny and Joon was the last thing on my mind. Benny and Joon had been responsible for everything wrong in my life. Because of that band, I was in a new city, with no friends, with parents who barely noticed my existence. Now I wanted my *own* band.

That's right. I wanted to rebel against my parents by doing *exactly* what they do. Weird, but true.

"Chocolate chip pancakes, anyone?" said Jake, pulling out a mixing bowl.

"Yes!" cried X, oblivious to the fact that this would be the third time Shaky Jake's pancakes had been on the menu that week. What normal family eats pancakes for dinner?

Rock stars' families eat pancakes for dinner.

JONNY

I was already late for Mr. V's class on Friday, but I put up the sign anyway. So far, the Band Formation Plan wasn't working. I had gotten the lay of the land. I had observed. But I hadn't caught even a whiff of another actual musician. I kept hearing about Raising Cain and some supposed riot-girl group called Mad Unicorn. But nobody else seemed to be interested in putting together a *new* band. I had to step it up.

I pulled out some thumbtacks and put my sign in the most conspicuous spot I could find on the activities board.

FOR THOSE ABOUT TO ROCK, I SALUTE YOU.
I'M ANNABELLE CABRERA,
AND I'M FORMING A ROCK BAND.
I PLAY BASS AND SING.
WHAT DO YOU PLAY?!?

LET'S JAM AND SEE WHAT HAPPENS.
P.S. I'M USUALLY WEARING A BEATLES HOODIE.

It was kind of embarrassing standing up on a table and getting that prickly-hairs-on-the-back-of-my-neck feeling that meant people were staring at me. But I needed something to happen.

☆

Mr. V leaned against his desk holding a big blue mixing bowl. His eyes were twinkling even more than usual. Something was up.

"Okay, this will be a bit more interesting, I hope, than reading assessments and grammar exercises," he said. "Today we will become writers. We will learn to craft a work of art."

The idiots in the back groaned.

"Here's a work of art," a boy named McNamara said, making a fart noise with his mouth.

But Mr. V had my attention. Ever since meeting Ronaldo, an amazing writer, I had been trying to write. Songs, of course. I carried a pocket-sized notebook around with me like Ronaldo did. I jotted down lyric ideas, but they usually didn't amount to much more than titles. I had lots of song *ideas*, but I didn't have any actual *songs*.

V stood up and displayed his mixing bowl, tilting it so the class could see. There were dozens of little slips of paper inside with words scrawled on them.

"Writing is a simple but elusive art," he said. "To write is to describe. Describe accurately and respectfully. And perhaps passionately."

Kissy sounds from the back.

"Not that kind of passion, Mr. McNamara, although good writers can expect to attract ample attention from the opposite sex, if that's what you meant to express. May I continue? Thank you so very much."

McNamara slumped in his seat, embarrassed.

"Inside this bowl there are many assignments for a budding writer. Some of the topics are concrete and very simple, like the description of an object. Other assignments are more . . . complicated. You will see what I mean by this. Every Monday until Christmas break, each of you will reach into this bowl and pick a topic. And every Friday you will hand in some writing about this topic."

"*Every* Friday?" asked McNamara.

"Yes, although you will be pleased to know that your writing may be of any length. If it takes you five words to describe your subject, and you choose the perfect five words, you will receive a good grade. If you write five silly words, or five ridiculous paragraphs, one might surmise that you are not trying your hardest. And students who do not try their hardest sometimes do not receive excellent grades."

Of course, as Mr. V passed out assignments, all the dorks in the back row announced their topic to the class as loudly as possible.

"What do you think your life will be like in ten years!"

"If you could have two famous people over for the day, who would it be and what would you do with them!" Snickers all around.

"Should we continue to fund the NASA space program!"

My heart started to race as Mr. V came closer with his

mixing bowl. Maybe I'd get a song out of this! I closed my eyes and fished around in the bowl for a couple seconds.

"Don't be afraid, Ms. Cabrera. Just pick one."

I grabbed a slip of paper, opened my eyes, and saw this:

"Write about a time when you were very homesick."

I looked up at Mr. V, who was raising his eyebrows, eyes doing that gleaming thing. Was this a trick? Could he have planted this on me? No way. There were still dozens of slips of paper in there.

How was I going to get a song out of this assignment? Missing Brooklyn, missing Egg Mountain, missing my *abuela*— that was pretty much all I thought about at this point. I would need a book the size of *David Copperfield* to get it all down.

☆

In the hall, Curly Burly passed by me so closely that we almost touched. He had switched his Mastodon T-shirt for one that said "If You Don't Fear God . . ." on the front. I made sure not to *make eye contact*, but I looked back when I felt it was safe and saw that the shirt read "Then Fear the METAL" on the back. Why are so many metal fans religious? I looked up at the ceiling and thanked my own higher power that Curly Burly hadn't noticed me. A few feet farther I noticed that same small blond kid sitting in front of his locker. He wasn't crying or anything, but his hair was all mussed and he wore a totally blank expression. He had obviously just given up his money again.

"Hey," I said.

"Hey," he said back.

"You all right?"

He just shrugged, looking down. I guess he didn't make eye contact with *anybody* anymore.

"Does that guy take your money every day?" I asked. I noticed he had a hilarious pair of sneakers on, with bright yellow and black stripes on them. It looked like he had two fat bumblebees for shoes. They didn't exactly match his mood.

"Yeah. It's not always him, though," he said. "There's three or four of them."

"Why don't you tell somebody? Like a teacher."

He sighed. "I know you're trying to be nice. But you're not helping. If I tell anyone, then they'll *really* get me. Just leave me alone, okay?"

"Okay, okay." So I moved on.

I know I claimed not to care about making friends, but I was doing a more spectacular job of it than I'd ever imagined possible. Even the lowest kids on the totem pole wanted nothing to do with me. They'd have to make a new table at the caff, one even more loserish than Loner Land. I'd be the only one sitting there, and during lunch all the other kids could throw pies at me or something.

I'm not sure if the same higher power that let me pass by Curly Burly without being seen could hear the self-pity session I was conducting in my head, but my luck was about to change. My *life* was about to change. I was about to meet Jonny.

I heard music—actual, nonrecorded, live-in-the-flesh music coming out of an empty classroom. The door was closed but not locked. I turned the knob to the right as slowly and carefully as I could so that I didn't just barge in on whoever was in there. As I pushed the door open about two inches, I saw a boy sitting on a desk playing an acoustic guitar. At first, I couldn't hear him above the hallway noise, but his lips were moving, so he had to be singing. Luckily, the boy had his back turned to me, so I was able to stick my whole head inside the room. Now I could hear him.

I totally knew the melody, but I couldn't figure out what the song was at first. My brain was in that frustrating place between knowing the tune and being able to actually name it. I scrunched my face in concentration, trying to figure it out.

Of course. It was "Crimson and Clover," one of my favorite songs ever! Tommy James and The Shondells sang it in the sixties, but my favorite version was by Joan Jett, my number two rock 'n' roll idol of all time (just behind Satomi). Joan sang it so softly and sweetly, but with the craziest metal-sounding guitars booming like thunder underneath. I remembered my dad once singing "Crimson and Clover" at an all-ages show in a Williamsburg record store. My mom had joined in on the words "what a beautiful feeling," and I could remember the way she had looked at him while they harmonized, as if he were some kind of god. It was over the top, almost gross—people don't want to see that kind of smoochie-boochie stuff at a rock show—but that's just how they are together. My mom is totally into my dad and my dad is totally into whatever song he's singing.

I kept watching. This kid wouldn't have been out of place in Loner Land, and I couldn't exactly imagine gazing dreamily into his eyes. He was big, but not in an athletic way. He had on a giant black parka, but I could still tell he was pretty hefty. He could stand to lose a few pounds. On top of that, he had big square-rimmed glasses that he pushed back to the top of his nose every five seconds because they kept sliding down.

The song sounded good, though, and I was impressed that this geeky kid got away with it. In my old school, for anybody but the most popular kids to display artistic talent, even in this semipublic setting, would have been like throwing a bloody leg to a pool of great whites. This kid, obviously not popular, an outcast for sure based on appearance alone, was taking a pretty large risk. Could he possibly just not care what anybody thought?

I could see that he had some real potential as a musician. He wasn't doing anything flashy on the guitar, but he had a good sense of rhythm, and a voice all his own: a little reedy, but gritty and solid. He wasn't going to win *American Idol* anytime soon, but there was a rocker budding inside him. When he was finished, I gave the door a little knock.

"Sorry to interrupt," I said. "Great song."

"Umm, thanks," he said. He stood up and gave me a major nerd stare, like he was having some trouble getting me into focus. Confused, he sat back down again. I walked toward him and sat on a nearby desk.

"Where'd you learn it?"

"My dad taught it to me."

"Really? My dad plays that song, too."

No response. He just pushed up his glasses.

"Well, I play bass, and I want to start a band, and—"

"And . . . you're new here, aren't you?"

"Yeah. Is it that obvious?"

"Providence is a small city, and the music scene's even smaller. If you weren't new, we'd already know each other."

"Yeah, that makes sense."

"I used to be in a band." He strummed a chord.

"And?"

"And . . . it didn't really go that well."

He actually seemed to think I would let it go at that.

"Umm, okay. Keep going . . ."

"It was with some guys who just turned out to be serious jerks." He played a power chord and held it. "I'm into playing alone now."

"What do you mean? Jerks how?"

"I don't know, just jerks."

"Okay." I rubbed my chin. "Well, what if it was with cooler people, wouldn't you want to be in a band again?"

"Probably not. I don't know." He was pretty good at creating an awkward vibe.

"So what's your name?"

"Jonny." Another power chord, even louder. "Really, I don't get why it always has to be about *bands*. Bands are like the big thing now. Everybody all of a sudden has to be in a *band*. But music doesn't always have to be about rocking out."

"What do you mean? Of course music is about rocking out!"

"I dunno."

"Nobody can rock alone, you must know that. Where would Paul McCartney be without John Lennon? Thom Yorke without Jonny Greenwood? Chuck D without Flava Flav?"

That got a laugh, so I decided to keep going.

"You want to be a *solo artist*? You want to be the next Justin Timberlake? Bright Eyes? Miley Cyrus, maybe?"

"Ha, Miley. What's your name, then, Miss Bandleader?"

"Annabelle Cabrera," I said, holding my hand out to him.

"Well, Annabelle Cabrera, today has been a weird one."
We shook hands. "First few days of school, and I just kind of
wish I was still sitting in my bedroom, playing guitar. You
know what I mean?"

I nodded. "My favorite part of the day is spent with my
bass and my iPod, learning songs."

"Exactly. And I'd like to keep it that way." He got up from
his chair. "But there *are* a bunch of musicians in this school."

"Yeah? I haven't had much luck."

"You just need to know where to look. I can help you, if
you want."

"For real?"

"Sure. Meet me here on Monday, same time. I'll give you a
little tour around."

Yes! A Federal Hill rock 'n' roll tour guide. I was on my way.
Rock stars hang out with other rock stars.

FRIED CHEESE AND SALAMI

I checked e-mail at home and saw one from Ronaldo. The subject line read "Ronaldo's Rules to Rock By." This is what it said:

1. Find the right bandmates. Form a band with your friends. It's better to have a pretty good drummer who's the coolest guy in the world than a great drummer who's a jerk.

2. Practice. Every great band practices tons. Whether your music's crazy-complicated or stupid-simple, you have to rehearse. Radiohead does it. So did The Ramones. And so will you.

3. Write. I know you keep your notebook. That's awesome. Keep going with it. Don't worry about saying anything

brilliant or earth-shattering. Write about things that mean something to you, and people will listen.

4. Record. Recording is really the last step of writing. You have no idea how much you'll learn about *writing* songs by *recording* them. You'll tear your hair out trying to capture THE perfect version of a song, and you'll probably rewrite the whole thing three or four times along the way. But you'll improve as a songwriter, and your band will get better and better, too.

5. Gig. It doesn't matter if you're playing at Madison Square Garden or the pizza place around the corner. Every gig will make you stronger as a band. Especially at the beginning, don't turn down gigs because they seem uncool. If your history teacher asks you to play for her dad and his checkers partner at the old folks' home, say yes.

Before I'd even finished reading, Ronaldo popped up on IM.

EggMtnRckr: so, did U get em?
Bassinyrface: sure did. thanks.
EggMtnRckr: and? what did you think?
Bassinyrface: well, I think I pretty much knew that stuff already. I mean, practice, write, record, gig? Duh.
EggMtnRckr: Maybe. But you'd be surprised how easy it is to forget the basics sometimes.
Bassinyrface: Ok. I DO have a question,

though . . . like, you say to form a band with my friends, but I dont really HAVE any friends here, remember?

EggMtnRckr: Maybe just make sure you pick bandmates that seem like they COULD be your friends.

Bassinyrface: yeah, that makes sense.

EggMtnRckr: just dont pick anybody who seems totally evil!

Bassinyrface: word. So i might have found a guitar player. MIGHT have. plays great but says he wants to stay solo.

EggMtnRckr: hmm . . . work on him.

Bassinyrface: What do you mean? How?

EggMtnRckr: He's prolly just shy. Nobody REALLY wants to do this alone. Just get to know him a little, and maybe he'll change his mind.

Bassinyrface: how did you find the egg guys?

EggMtnRckr: they came to me.

Bassinyrface: shaddup YOU were the one who came to ME.

EggMtnRckr: Yeah but U were a special case, Annabelle. ☺ The other guys found me. The most important thing is, you gotta find people you like as people, cuz you'll be spending a lotta time together. U know?

Bassinyrface: Are you saying I need to be more likable?

EggMtnRckr: No I'm saying . . . be YRSELF.

Bassinyrface: Meh.

EggMtnRckr: Hey, I like you so at least you've got THAT, annabelle.

Bassinyrface: Ha, thanks, R. U are awesome.

☆

As it turned out, I had a chance to work on my writing later that very night. I lay on my bed, stomach-down, a couple sheets of paper in front of me and a pen in my hand.

"Write about a time when you were very homesick," read the assignment.

Ugh. I was homesick right *now*. Did Mr. V make up this homework just for me, or what? Missing my old city was about the last thing in the world I wanted to put into words at that moment, so I tried to think of the assignment as Coming Up with Ideas for Future Songs, not as having anything to do with school.

Rock stars don't do homework, I thought.

But they do write songs—or at least they try to.

Everything was better in Brooklyn, I wrote.

I looked at the sentence, and kind of liked it. Could it be a lyric? Maybe. I decided to just write a bunch of sentences as fast as they came to me.

I miss fried cheese and salami.
I miss soccer games in Red Hook Park.
I miss my abuela.

Everything *had* been better in Brooklyn. For one thing, Abuela, my grandmother on my dad's side, the Dominican side, had always been around. It was actually Abuela's apartment that we had lived in right up until the move to Providence. We had never had a place all to ourselves before. My dad had never really left home, except for an apartment in Prospect Heights, where he lasted for about five minutes without Abuela's home-cooked meals. When my parents got married, my mom had moved in, and then they had me and X.

There was never any guessing whose house it was, though. Abuela was the queen of the castle. That is, if a queen worked really hard all day long in a housecoat and slippers. And if the castle were a dingy three-bedroom apartment in Sunset Park. Even with my mom and dad supposedly in charge of X and me, it was pretty clear who called the shots at Abuela's house.

Abuela had earned the right to tell us what to do. While my parents raced from gig to gig or slept off a late-night recording session, Abuela was at home doing what needed to be done. She was the one, not my parents, who walked X and me to the bus every morning. She was the one who came to soccer games with tasty treats for all my teammates and slowly, methodically opened our report cards as soon as they arrived in the mail. She would force us to stand right in front of her as she did it, too. When the grades were good, Abuela would go nuts baking cakes or cookies or a pie, feeding us until we were about to explode. When they were not so good, she'd get all serious and say, "I know you do better next time."

Abuela used to get up every day at sunrise and make *café con leche* for herself with her hair curlers still on. She tore off bits of bread and dunked them in the coffee, always taking a moment to savor the taste. Only once had I actually been awake early enough to see her make breakfast. Usually the smell of hot food was already in the air by the time I even opened my eyes, the pots and pans having long been cleaned and put away.

But one time, when I was about eight, I was sick with a fever. I woke up when it was still dark out, and I was scared. I wandered, sleepy and spaced out, into the kitchen, my blanket trailing behind me. Standing in the kitchen door, I watched Abuela doing her thing. She was making my favorite, fried cheese and salami with a side of *casabe*, a cracker made from yucca. It was 90 percent grease, and it tasted amazing.

Abuela had made this dish at least twice a week for my whole life, but she always took it really seriously, like she was making it for the first time. She was obsessed with getting the fried cheese just right: it had to be golden and crispy on the bottom, and if she didn't feel it was perfect, she'd throw the whole thing out and start over. She would squint at the pan and lift it from the fire, then have a staring contest with the browned edges of the cheese. That day, it was ready. It was just right. She plated two portions for X and me, not realizing I was standing right behind her. When I coughed into my blanket, she spotted me and jumped back, surprised.

"Oh, baby, you scare me," she said, pulling out a chair. "Sit down. Eat."

Now I sat in a huge, humid apartment in a new city, and I hadn't had cheese and salami for over two months. And what was for dinner tonight in the Cabrera household? Shaky Jake's chocolate chip pancakes again—I could almost bet on it. X would be on a three-hour sugar high, as usual. While Jake ruled in many ways, he was no Abuela. He couldn't hold our family together while my parents lived in their fantasy world.

Was I homesick? I felt like I didn't *have* a home anymore. Home was something we had left in Sunset Park. Now I was living in a recording studio, which is the exact opposite of a home.

I looked at what I had written, pulled out a rhyming dictionary, and started to screw around:

> Everything's better in Brooklyn
> Fried salami, goopy cheese
> Egg Mountain shows and the East River
>   breeze
> Take me back to Brooklyn, please
>
> Man, I miss my old hometown
> Milk shakes at Uncle Louie G's
> What's for dinner tonight, pizza or
>   Chinese?
> Take me back to Brooklyn, please

What are you going to make of my masterpiece, Mr. V?

☆

"What's up, Cabrera?" Jonny said on the following Monday. He was waiting for me at the empty classroom at lunchtime, right where he said he'd be.

"Not much, Jonny . . ." I waited for him to fill in the blank. But he didn't.

"Just Jonny."

"Okay, Jonny No Last Name. Jonny Mysterious."

"Ha, it's Jonny Mack."

"Pleased to meet you, Mr. Mack."

"Likewise."

We were both brown-bagging it, so we skipped the caff and walked through the halls. I hadn't been this near him standing upright before, so it was like I was looking at him for the first time. Dyed black hair with bangs long enough to cover a slightly patchy forehead. A small white scar above his lip. Black T-shirt, black jeans, black Chuck high-tops. Next to him, I looked like Little Miss Sunshine. He was way more goth than I remembered, like the doofus big brother to that *David Copperfield*–obsessed pixie I'd seen in Loner Land.

"I can't believe your parents are Benny and Joon," he said. "*Entranced* is a great record."

"You Googled me?"

"Yup." He pushed up his glasses.

"All righty, then."

"So are they crazy? Why would you guys leave Brooklyn? Brooklyn is like the international center of indie rock."

"Tell me about it. Shows every night of the week."

"All my favorite bands are from Brooklyn. Animal Collective, Liars, Interpol, they're all there."

"I know."

"You must be bummed. There's maybe ten bands in all of Providence, and half of them are metal tribute bands."

"Yeah."

"So . . . why'd you move here, then?"

"My parents wanted a place where they could live and record, and they couldn't afford it in Brooklyn."

"Really? But they're totally successful."

"Well, if by 'successful' you mean that a lot of people like them, sure. But they don't exactly rake cash in, doing what they do. They're not competing with Beyoncé for a spot on the top ten."

"Well, yeah, they're indie. But they could play to at least five hundred people in almost every major city in the country. Not Providence, maybe, but every *major* city."

"Yeah, I guess. But you'd be surprised how little they make, after you count up the hotel bills, the gas, the blah, blah, blah. They don't make much on records, either."

"Oh man, that sucks. I guess I should listen to my dad and become a lawyer, then?"

"Ha. Totally, you traitor."

We walked by my poster, and Jonny stopped.

"This is you, right?"

I nodded.

"'For those about to rock'?" he read.

"Umm, yeah. You think that was cheesy?"

"Nah, don't worry about it. Everybody needs a little cheese in their diet. So what do you think, are you gonna form the biggest band in the world, or what?"

"Well, you've gotta start somewhere, right?"

"What's more important? Is it about being incredibly popular, or just sounding really amazing?"

I had to think about it. "When I imagine this band," I said, "we're playing in front of thousands of people. But for thousands of people to like us, we'd have to sound really great, right?"

"Yeah, but there are some really, really popular bands whose music is terrible, don't you think? Look at Hilary Duff."

"Well, sure, I hate ninety-nine percent of what's on the radio. So I guess I want to be the biggest *and* the best."

"So, Annabelle Cabrera has to have it all."

Heh. I was starting to like this guy. We kept walking.

As we made our way toward the yard, I realized we were getting an awful lot of sidelong glances. I couldn't figure out why. A pudgy goth nerd taking a stroll with a four-foot-ten rock girl. *Keep moving, people,* I thought. *Nothing to see here.*

Suddenly, I saw a familiar face: the attention-deficit girl from the week before. She walked right next to me, talking to one of her friends in a voice obviously meant to be overheard by anybody within a mile radius.

"There she is, the talent scout," she said nastily. "The choir director who thinks she's too good for this school."

I winced. "Don't ask," I whispered to Jonny. "ADHDiva."

She went left, thankfully, and we went right.

Jonny pushed open the door to the yard with his shoulder.

"Ah, fresh air," he said. "Too stuffy in that hallway."

We rested our backs against the wall, squinted into the sun, and pulled out our lunches. I was having another one of Jake's specialties, PB&J. Jonny chomped on a tangerine, a Ho Ho, and a piece of mayo-slathered salami that he had pulled out of a soggy-looking sandwich.

"Nice feast," I said.

"Ho Hos rock."

Three big guys walked by. My eyes were at jeans level, and I spotted a folded Fender guitar strap hanging out of one of the dudes' back pockets. Keeping in mind Jonny's anti-band attitude and Ronaldo's very first rule to rock by, I got up and started following them.

"Annabelle, wait up," Jonny said. "Bad idea!"

But I was already off and running.

I followed the jeans until I could get a better view of the kid wearing them. He was massive, adult-tall, with slicked-back hair and the beginnings of a scraggly goatee. He had on the mirrored sunglasses of a cop and a swimmer's broad shoulders. Had to be an eighth grader. I walked alongside him until he couldn't ignore me anymore.

Finally, he stopped and faced me.

"What?" he said. His buddies turned around, and I immediately recognized one of them as Curly Burly. Disaster. But it was too late. I was on the spot now.

"You . . . play guitar?"

"You . . . know who you're talking to?" the guy said in a voice unbelievably deep for a middle schooler. He turned to Jonny, who had just caught up to us and was so out of breath he had to put his hands on his knees to keep from hyperventilating. "Fatty McGoth, you want to introduce me to this . . . Muppet?"

"Annabelle . . . this is Jackson Royer," Jonny said. "Jackson, this is Annabelle. She's, um, a bass player, and she's starting a band." Jonny stuttered a bit and kept his eyes on the floor.

"Thanks for the translation," Jackson said, smirking. He peered out from the top of his sunglasses and looked me up and down so slowly that I could feel my flesh crawl. Somehow, I still had time to wonder how much hair product it took to keep a slickie like his going all day long. Once we got super friendly, I'd have to ask him.

"What are you going to do, Beatles Girl—sing 'She Loves You' and 'I Want to Hold Your Hand' until McGoth lets you be his girlfriend?"

"Ha-ha, Jackson. Hilarious," Jonny said.

"I thought it was amusing, myself," Jackson said. "Jonny, remind your new lady friend: no eye contact."

I could feel my face go red. The heat started in my neck and spread across my entire face in about a half second. I tried to say something, but the words died on their journey up my throat. Jackson turned toward Jonny, took off the shades, and looked at the scar above his lip like a doctor examining a patient.

"It's healing quite nicely," Jackson said, walking away. "Good luck with your little project, Beatles Girl!"

"Annabelle, maybe you should slow things down a little," Jonny said. "I was about to tell you, number one, that Jackson's already *in* a band, and that, number two—"

"Why did he say your scar's healing nicely?"

"Nothing. Forget it."

"Did that guy give you the scar?"

"I said forget it."

"Okay, fine. So there's *another* band at Federal Hill?" I said.

"Yeah, there's Jackson's band, Raising Cain. They're heavy. They're all eighth graders. And they're really good."

"So I've heard. What grade are you in anyway? You're sixth, right?"

"Seventh. But I occasionally allow sixth graders to talk to me." A quick smile. "Anyway, listen. Even more important is that Jackson Royer is easily the biggest jerk in the whole school. There's no point in talking to him. He'll just mess with your head."

"Okay, I get the message."

Here's a new rule to rock by, I thought.

Rock stars don't let bullies mess with their heads.

The Church of Rock

"Hey ho, let's go!" Xavier shouted the next Saturday morning, processed sugar pumping through his veins. He was skateboarding wildly inside the house, although for once it was for a very specific reason. See, a miracle had taken place: my dad had agreed to take some time off from mixing the Benny and Joon album, and the Cabreras were going on . . . a family outing.

"Nick, honey, have you seen the blanket?" my mom asked.

"Babe, we're not going camping," said Dad. "We're just going for a walk. Right?"

"I thought we could go to Roger Williams Park. It's supposed to be beautiful there. I packed lunches."

"Roger Williams Park! Roger Williams Park! Roger Williams Park!" X chanted.

"I said I could take a couple hours off, not the whole day," Dad said.

"Whole day off, whole day off!" X had obviously entered a chanting phase, and it was grating on all of our nerves. My nine-year-old brother was starting to act six again. Or maybe five? Not cool. Not cool at all.

"Nick," Mom said, "can I talk to you for a second . . . in private?"

I had to laugh at that one. There was no such thing as "in private" in our place. Unless they were going to lock themselves in the bathroom and whisper like church mice, X and I would hear every word.

My mom took my dad's elbow and steered him toward the kitchen. They actually did a pretty good job, because I just heard a few snippets.

". . . almost finished with it . . . ," said Dad.

". . . but that was the whole point . . . ," Mom said.

". . . what puts food on the table . . ."

". . . not about the money and you know it . . ."

". . . come to a compromise . . ."

"Okay, okay."

". . . I'll do my best . . . you know I love you . . ."

"Yes I do . . . now where is that blanket?"

Mom walked back toward us. "Okay, kids, we've got it all figured out. We're going to take a walk over to Brown. We'll do a little window shopping, maybe get some ice cream—"

"J and J's Candy Bar, J and J's Candy Bar!" X chanted the name of a great ice cream place on Thayer Street, one we passed every time we went into town, as he literally tried to run up a wall.

"Xavier, honey, you need to calm down, okay?" Mom said.

"Sugar is the last thing X needs," my dad said, but he said it nicely, ruffling X's hair and giving him a playful swat on the butt. I could tell X was glad to have my dad's attention, but it didn't calm him down at all. If anything, it revved him up even more.

On the way out the door, Mom tried to take X's hand, but he twisted out of her grip. He zipped down the staircase, sliding on the handrail like a maniac. So we had it all: parental tension *and* my brother dancing on the edge of chaos in the key of fourth grade.

X had never been this bad in Brooklyn. Sure, he had always been a sugar freak. He could get out of control like any nine-year-old. And my parents were horrible at controlling him. But Abuela and I had always been able to calm him down, and when he *was* mellow, he was an incredibly cool guy. He was hilarious at imitations, he was a great dancer, and he had a ridiculous memory for baseball statistics. How many nine-year-olds do you know who can do the moonwalk while reciting Albert Pujols's slugging percentage for the last five seasons?

X was really sweet and considerate, too. Since age four he'd been making his own presents for the whole family on Christmas and birthdays. He'd spend a whole day making cards and collages out of whatever materials he could find in the house: glue, tinsel, toy soldiers, jigsaw pieces, spices from Abuela's cabinets. But ever since the move all he seemed to want to do was blabber nonsense, skate inside the house,

and generally annoy the bejesus out of everybody in sight.
I hadn't had an actual conversation with him in weeks.
Nobody had.

☆

"What a gorgeous day. I feel like I haven't been outside in
ages," my mom said, apparently trying to steer the SS *Cabrera*
toward some friendlier waters.

Dad was a half block in front of us, trying to keep up
with X.

"You haven't," I said. "You're making a record. It's always
like this when you're making a record."

"You're right. It's been too long. Too long since I've spent
any time with my daughter, too." She tousled my hair. "How
were your first couple weeks of school?"

"Do you really want to know? This is the first time since
school started that you've talked to me for more than two
minutes."

"Baby, I'm sorry." She stopped. "Belle?"

I stopped after a few feet, and she walked toward me. She
reached out, about to touch my shoulder, then pulled back.

"Belle, I promise that things will go back to normal . . .
some kind of normal . . . when this record is done. I know
this move's been hard on you, and I want you to know that I
know that. It's been hard for me and your dad, too." Did Dad
even notice what state he was in when he was this obsessed?
"We'll all get through this, I promise. So . . . will you tell me
how Federal Hill is?"

"It's okay, I guess."

I walked on, head down, trying to decide if I was going to

let her off this easy. The weird thing is that if I had been in her position, with my band and a new recording studio at my beck and call, I wouldn't want to be the typical parent, either. I'd just want to be in the studio all day, dreaming up new songs, new sounds.

"Okay, how?"

"I mean in some ways it might be even worse than Sunset Park."

"What ways?"

"It's just thug boys playing tough and girls in halter tops. Rock is dead."

"Well, give it time. You trying to find people to play music with?"

"Yeah. Trying. It's hard, though."

Up ahead, I saw X swinging monkey-style on my dad's right bicep. Dad turned around and gave my mom a pleading look. She ignored it.

"It's never easy, finding people you like *and* like to play with. Before your dad, I just went from band to band to band. Nothing ever clicked."

"Tell me the story again? How you guys met?"

"Again?"

"Come on. I like it."

I knew that I was still supposed to be mad at my mom. But it was just easier to let her off the hook, and I *wanted* the story. I needed it. It gave me hope. If Mom had conquered Ronaldo's first rule of rock, so would I.

"I've told you that story a thousand times."

She brushed back her hair and smiled. It was true. I was always asking her to tell me the story of how Benny and Joon came to be. I couldn't help it. It was like the best VH1 *Behind the Music* ever. It was romantic *and* it was about rock 'n' roll.

"Okay, okay . . . It was a little over thirteen years ago. The grunge years. I had just moved to New York from Ohio, and I didn't know a soul. I used to get up, get a Vietnamese coffee from this little place in the East Village, and grab the *Village Voice*. This was before the Internet was really that big, so musicians put ads in the *Voice* when they were looking for band members. Your dad's ad definitely stood out."

"What'd it say?"

"You've probably got it memorized by now, I've told this story so many times."

"Come on, just tell it right."

"It said, 'Kurt Cobain's guitars are hurting my eardrums. Let's hide out in my room and play pretty records. Sick-of-it-all singer/guitar player seeks bass and drums.' "

"But you play keyboards."

"I just liked the ad, and I went for it. I showed up at his apartment . . . it was right around the corner from me. I didn't know what to expect. I thought he might be a ninety-pound weakling who hadn't seen sunlight in years. I didn't know if he'd be able to play—I didn't know whether the man would be able to hold a conversation. But I was curious. I couldn't not go."

"So what did you think when you first saw him?"

"Well, it took him a long time to answer the door, I'll tell you that much. And when he did, he looked like he hadn't been sleeping very well. He hadn't shaved in a couple of days, and he was wearing a white V-neck T-shirt with yellow stains under the armpits."

"Gross!"

"Yeah, maybe. But he was so sweet. And innocent, like a little boy . . ."

This I didn't get. What's cute about a guy who acts like a little kid?

"He was holding a to-go coffee cup, and the first thing he did when he saw me was spill it on his jeans."

"More stains."

"Yeah, more stains. As soon as he recovered, he realized that I was still carrying my keyboard on my shoulder, so he put his coffee down and helped me get it into his apartment. The place was so tiny. And dirty. He was sharing it with I don't know how many other musicians, and they never cleaned the place. There were dishes in the sink that must have been in there for months."

"Wait, I can take it from here," I said.

"Okay. Go for it." My mom laughed.

"Then he pulled out his guitar and played you a really beautiful song. He had been writing songs since he was sixteen and he'd never really played them for anyone else, so he was super nervous. But you just sat there, and you crushed out on him *and* the songs he was playing. You started to play along. He liked what you were doing, and he asked you if you could sing. You started to harmonize, and it was awesome. You were just looking at each other like, *Is this a dream?* Then, after an hour or so, he just leaned over and kissed you like you had known each other forever. Like it was nothing. And then a year later I was born."

She laughed. "It wasn't quite that simple, but yes, we did get serious right away. We didn't think about it at all. We just went for it."

See, my mom can be pretty cool when she wants to be. I just wish she wanted to be a little more often.

My dad was waiting for us by the time we got to Thayer Street. I tried to picture him the way my mom must have seen him back then. He was still unshaven, still obsessed with music. But he didn't seem like someone who would lean over and kiss somebody he'd met an hour earlier. He just seemed tired and cranky.

"Okay, babe, it's tag-team time. I need a break."

X had already run ahead of him by a block and was waiting with puppy dog eyes in front of J & J's Candy Bar.

"The kid is pretty whacked today," Dad said. "You sure ice cream's a good idea?"

"It's my fault. For mentioning it at home," my mom said.

We gathered at the shop, ordered ice creams—sugar free for X, not that it made a noticeable difference—and kept moving.

"Should we say hi to Don?" I asked.

"Perfect," Dad said. "Don loves X. Maybe he can surrogate-parent for us."

I had been planning for this possibility while my mom was telling the origin myth. We needed a tension breaker. And we couldn't take a stroll down Thayer Street and *not* enter the Church of Rock, known to mortals as Don Daddio's Guitars.

☆

"I didn't know you guys ever traveled as a pack," said Don Daddio as we walked into the store. Three or four guys were hunched over guitars, playing loudly and not very well. It was always like this at Don's, a mini-orchestra of mediocre guitar players competing for attention.

"What's up, Don?" I said.

"I might not be thrivin', but I'm survivin'," Don said. He held his hand out for X, who ran up and smacked out the hardest low five he could.

"Whoa, this guy is building his strength," Don said.

"Belle, hang out with me," X said, tugging on my hand.

"I will, bud. In a sec. Why don't you go to the drum room"— it was his favorite room in the shop—"and I'll meet you there in a little bit."

"Okay, in a *little* little bit," X said, running off.

"Phew," my dad said. "He is off the rails today."

"So, what brings you here, Nick?" asked Don. "You break another D string?"

"No, I'm good, string-wise. We're just having a—a family day." My dad couldn't even spit out this simple sentence without stuttering.

When we first arrived in Providence two months ago and my parents were building the studio, we took countless trips to Don's. Mom and Dad had also said we could hang out at the shop while they were recording, so we'd already spent tons of time there.

The first thing anyone noticed about Don Daddio was The Hair. Although the *top* of Don's head was well on the road to Bald Mountain, he still had a thick mane of dark corkscrew curls that reached all the way down his back. Sometimes he wore The Hair in a ponytail, but today he had on his Don Daddio's baseball hat and the corkscrews puffed out the sides of the cap like fat angel wings. His big belly pushed up against a T-shirt that read "Born a Rocker, Die a Rocker." Don was a chubbed-out metal guy who didn't seem at all bummed that he was several years past his prime.

"And what can I do *you* for, Belle?" Don asked.

A squeal of feedback screamed out of a nearby amplifier. Don winced.

"*Ay ay ay.* Excuse me one sec, hon," he said, waddling swiftly toward the offender, an impossibly skinny white boy with long, spindly legs and a T-shirt that read "One Day I'll Be Your Boss." Don put his hand on the fret board of the screaming guitar, and the kid looked up, surprised.

"Dylan, buddy, you're killing me here. The Daddios are hard of hearing as it is. You wanna make me deaf before I hit forty-five?"

The kid looked at Don like he was speaking Swahili. I heard some noise in the back of the shop. X was making a real racket in the percussion room.

"If you want to turn it up to eleven, you gotta do that at home, okay, kid?"

The boy nodded sleepily, and Don returned to his perch behind the counter, rolling his eyes.

"You tell him, Don," Mom said.

"Thank ya much, Leah," said Don. "Belle, I'm guessing you'd like a few minutes alone with that Beatle bass, eh? The Hofner?"

"Sure," I said. Duh. I love that bass. That's the bass Paul McCartney plays! The bass Satomi Matsuzaki from Deerhoof plays! That bass is my dream bass.

Don walked to the vintage wall, where his most precious instruments were displayed behind glass, and pulled it out.

"Excellent. The prodigious young Cabrera girl indulges her sixties obsession yet again."

There was a loud crash from the percussion room.

"What in God's name is that kid doing back there?" Don headed in that direction and my mom gave me a nervous smile.

With a silent apology to Satomi (my poor bass was sitting at home, and here I was, cheating in public), I plugged the Hofner into an old Ampeg amp. I figured that anything could happen with the mood X was in, so I'd better get my licks in now. That Beatle bass was so sweet! I played some riffs I'd been working on lately, originals, and each note sounded so rich and smooth. It was glorious.

"Dad, what do you think of this one?" I asked, playing a White Stripes–ish bass line that I thought could make a cool song. "Dad?" It was torture even trying to get him to listen. He wasn't even looking at guitars; he was just spacing.

"Oh yeah, Belle. That's nice. Sounds good."

"Thanks." Was he listening or not? This was the problem with Dad. He was pretty good at pretending to clue in—he could put a smile on and nod at all the right moments—but I had the feeling he barely heard a word I said.

Suddenly, another loud crash from the percussion room. "Oh boy, here we go," said my dad, going to investigate. I couldn't hear what was said after that, but he really looked like he was about to lose it when he entered the room. X had probably knocked some drums over or something, and Dad seemed like he was about to cry. My mom and I just stood there nervously. And before we knew it, there was another crash, followed by my dad letting out a truly pained sounding *"Owwww!"* Then X flew out of the room, zipped by me, and took refuge behind a Marshall stack.

"He threw a cymbal at my shin." My dad race-limped out, rolling up his pant leg to inspect the damage. I could see a welt was already forming. "This is family time? What did *I* do?"

Yep, that just about summed it up. Together time. Love and kisses. A family outing, Cabrera-style, complete with two kids who were angry beyond words and two parents who didn't seem to understand why. The only difference between X and me was that he had the courage to actually show how mad he was while I escaped into Beatles songs. I couldn't wait to get home and play my bass.

Rock stars just don't do family outings.

Haiku City

I went straight to my "room," pulled out my cell phone, and dialed Abuela's number. What would she have to say about the cold, high-ceilinged apartment, the mic stands left in the shower, my parents staying up all night, forgetting to tuck in X, forgetting even to make dinner most nights?

By the fourth ring, I knew she wasn't going to pick up. This was the hard thing about trying to call Abuela. She was *always* home, but she could never get to the phone before the old-school answering machine picked up. It was only six p.m., so I figured she was either doing the dishes, asleep in front of the TV, or blasting an old merengue CD on the boom box in her bedroom. Sure enough, the outgoing message started to play, the same one Abuela had kept on the machine my whole life. Abuela spoke loudly and at a slow pace that always used to drive me crazy when I'd call home. Tonight, though, I didn't mind. The thought of Abuela recording this years ago, probably reading and rereading the simple message a dozen times to get it right, made me smile.

"Joo have reach home of Marielis Eliana Cabrera . . . and her family also . . ." She sounded like she was yelling at a deaf person. "Please, now, you leave message for us. And . . . we will call you back . . . when we are no busy. Please speak slowly, and do not to leave a message too long. Good-bye."

"*Hola*, Abuela, it's me, Annabelle . . . are you there?" I yelled it, but I knew from experience how unlikely it was that Abuela would hear the message, now or ever. She rarely remembered to check the machine, and my parents and I would sometimes have to go through dozens of messages, one by one, when the tape filled up and the machine stopped working.

"Abuela, I hope you are doing good. X and I are okay. We both started school a couple weeks ago. There're only a few middle schools in Providence, so my school's way bigger than 443. Mom and Dad are busy with recording all the time. X is okay, I guess. Today he threw a cymbal at Dad. I would really love to talk to you right now. Do you have my cell? 718-215-1333. Call me if you can, okay? Love you, Abuela. Call me . . ."

☆

EggMtnRckr: Wait, WHY exactly did X throw a cymbal? Did he draw blood?

Bassinyrface: No, no . . . I mean, I'm sure it hurt, but my dad didnt go to the hospital or anything.

EggMtnRckr: What is goin on up there anyway? X is not exactly the cymbal thrower type.

Bassinyrface: well, he is since he moved HERE.

EggMtnRckr: sux that bad, eh?

Bassinyrface: Worse. I mean, my parents are never here. Remember how Abuela was always cooking like a crazy woman in my old house?

EggMtnRckr: yup, I do. it always smelled like onions frying in butter. And tomato sauce.

Bassinyrface: Well, my parents cant cook! And they dont clean, or anything. Abuela did EVERYTHING, and now she's not here to help us.

EggMtnRckr: Ugh, that blows. But maybe things will get better? Maybe your mom n dad can do that stuff? Or maybe you and X can.

Bassinyrface: My parents never do anything except record and tour. You know that.

EggMtnRckr: So Belle, how about YR band stuff? Any progress on the rules?

Bassinyrface: mmm, not really. But I did find out there's another band at school.

EggMtnRckr: Yeah? Any good?

Bassinyrface: Well they're just a cover band like us, at least I think. But I hear they rule.

EggMtnRckr: Cover bands never rule. Original songs do.

Bassinyrface: Yeah, but I've heard like three people at school say they totally rock your face off.

EggMtnRckr: Well, listen, dont let em scare you. Whatever they have in tightness, u can make up for with good ORIGINAL songs.

Bassinyrface: I know, Professor Duffy, that's what u always say.

EggMtnRckr: It's true, though! How's rule #3 coming?

Bassinyrface: My songwriting? Nothing to share . . . yet. But I'll keep you posted.

EggMtnRckr: you should. U R gonna be a genius, I can tell.

Bassinyrface: thanks, R. You always know what to say. But . . . does it always take this long to form a band? This is getting super annoying.

EggMtnRckr: Belle, you've just started. It can take months to find just the right people.

Bassinyrface: But it didnt with Egg Mountain. Right after I joined, we were totally dominating the city. We had fans, we had gigs.

EggMtnRckr: Ha, so U think yr the secret to my success, eh? You do realize we were a band for almost a year before you graced us with your presence?

Bassinyrface: uhh, yeah, I do. And no, I dont think I'm the reason we were popular.

EggMtnRckr: You were PART of it. But another part of it was all the work we did for the year before that. Cant tell you how many times we played to four people in a lame café.

Bassinyrface: really?

EggMtnRckr: So, try to be patient. It'll happen. Promise!!!

☆

After chatting with Ronaldo, I pulled out my homework. I had picked an especially ridiculous writing assignment out of the blue bowl this week: "Which of your personal traits would you most like to pass on to your children?"

I would have liked to write an essay on all the reasons that assignment was just plain wrong. After the incident at Don's, the last thing on my mind was my future family. Not *everybody* is going to have a million children anyway. And what if some girl in my class *does* want children in the future but can't have them for some medical reason? She'll remember the time in sixth grade when she was forced to describe the traits she wanted to pass on to her kids in some dumb essay, and she'll feel terrible. I wanted to protest this assignment for ethical reasons.

Luckily, Mr. V told us we could always write about something else if we didn't feel "inspired" by the one from the blue bowl. I tried some haikus:

Forced Family Fun
Drove us all bonkers today
Ice cream, salty tears

My dad loves music
My mom just follows my dad
Where do we fit in?

It seems clear to me
X chucked a cymbal at Dad!
He just needs some love

I need this rock band
To keep from going crazy
When will it happen?

Moments after I finished, my phone started to sing out The Beatles' "Eleanor Rigby." That was my customized Abuela ring!

I opened the flip cover. "Abuela?" I answered.

"Hola, mi Annabella," Abuela said. "How you, my baby? Tell Abuela."

I surprised myself by choking up with tears and almost not being able to talk.

"Annabella, is you all right?" Abuela asked.

I got it together. "Yeah, yeah, I'm good," I said, trying to keep my voice from sounding shaky. "I was just drinking something, and it went down the wrong pipe."

"Oh, I am sorry, angel. But you doing okay? Tell me. Why your brother throw a thimble at your papa?"

"A cymbal, Abuela—you know, like part of a drum set?"

"He what? Why he throw that? Why he hurt your papa?"

"Well, maybe because he's tired of being ignored."

"Your father ignore Chabito? Your mother?"

"Well, yeah. We're not exactly getting tons of attention right now."

"You want me talk to him? Talk to you father?"

"Well, maybe, but I don't know what good it'll do."

"What you mean? You mama and papa always be good for you, Annabella. Maybe lots of things happening for they music now, so they don't see. Maybe—Annabelle, what is wrong, baby? You crying?"

I totally was *not* crying when she asked. I was just sniffling for a half second. But the second she said the word "crying," I completely broke down, snorting and sniffing and choking on my own tears.

"Oh, baby, I'm so sorry. You cry with Abuela now, is okay. You feel better. You will."

Abuela had always been big on getting tears out of your system. She said you needed to cry to put out the fires in your life, and that when you stopped you could take a look at what had burned down, and what hadn't. So I just cried for a minute or two. Abuela was probably the only person in the world who I'd let see me like that. I knew it wouldn't change the way she looked at me, so it didn't matter. I just cried it out.

"You feel a little better, *angelita*?" Abuela asked.

"Yeah, a little," I said. "But I'm not really even that sad. I'm just . . . mad."

"At you fathers?" This was the word Abuela always said for *parents*, but I always smiled when I heard it, as if X and I were being raised by Charlie Sheen and his brother on *Two and a Half Men*.

"Yeah, mostly at them. But even at you a little, Abuela. This family doesn't work without you. Don't you get that?"

Now it was her turn to pretend not to cry. But I heard her breathe in sharply, and when she exhaled she sounded shaky.

"I'm sorry, baby," she managed to say. "I knew it would no be easy, but I no like to hear you like this."

I could tell I had gotten to her. "Are you still sure you'd never come up here and live with us?"

"Oh, baby, you know how much it hurt me not to have my babies with me in Brooklyn no more. But maybe you understand me more when you old. I move around so much in my life, Annabella, and lot of times, no so happy thing for me to move. Like when I come to *this* country, not easy. When I marry you *gran papi* and live with *him*, not so easy. I have all my *friends* here, all my old lady friends and my family."

"What do you mean? *We're* your family."

"Yes, yes, baby, for certain you are my family, my family most important. But I have my cousins and my sisters here, and they understand what it mean to be old lady like me, and how to help old lady like me. They can take care of your Abuela maybe better than you fathers take care. I never been to this Providence, this new city, and would be very *hard* for me to change now, to live there now."

"But I miss you!"

"I miss you, too, Annabella, you know I do. I come visit so soon, I promise you, okay?"

"Wait, hold on," I said. "Did you just say a second ago that you didn't come up here because you know Mom and Dad can't take care of you? Or *won't* take care of you?"

"Annabella, I know you think me so strong, but I not so healthy all time anymore. Is hard to get older. Consuela, she take care me, and your uncle Roberto. Your mommy and daddy, they too busy."

I suddenly realized what Abuela had obviously under-stood for a long time now: my parents weren't so hot at *parenting*. They had been okay while Abuela was young enough and strong enough to hold everything together. But she was getting old and needed rest. And my parents were in no con-dition to help anybody but themselves.

"Maybe X and I should have stayed in Brooklyn with you," I said. "Even though you're getting older, you could take care of us way better than they can."

"Annabella, no! I no like hear you speak this way, okay?

You must love you fathers, and respect them. Even though they not perfect. Even though they make you angry." She blew her nose, and I could picture her picking up one of the frilly baby blue handkerchiefs that she always carried around with her when she had a cold, hand-washing them with the rest of the laundry three times a week. "Life sometime very hard, baby, *very* hard. But you have to be strong. You got to be. And you got to remember that I love you, too, okay? Abuela love you *very* much."

"I love you, too, Abuela," I said, trying to ignore the voice inside my head that said, *You are not as strong as she is. Will you ever be?* "Very much."

CRACKERS 'N' CHEESE

Mr. V gave me back my "homesickness" assignment on the following Tuesday. It didn't have a grade, but it was covered in red marks.

Everything's better in Brooklyn
Fried salami, goopy cheese
Egg Mountain shows and the East River breeze
Take me back to Brooklyn, please

Man, I miss my old hometown
Milk shakes at Uncle Louie G's
What's for dinner tonight, pizza or Chinese?
Take me back to Brooklyn, please

Ms. Cabrera, a few comments:

- *Nice emotion in this piece*
- *What is the Egg Mountain?*
- *"Goopy cheese" is a nice colloquial phrase, which makes me very hungry.*
- *I want to know more. There is a great deal of greasy food in Providence as well, I'm sure you know. What else are you missing? Other places, other people? Can you write more verses, please?*
- *"Uncle Louie G's?" Is this the proper spelling? Please verify.*
- *"pizza or Chinese"—nice touch, celebrating multicultural cuisine*

This is a nice beginning. It begs questions of the reader, which is a good thing. Is it a poem or a song? Songs are a legitimate form—you should keep working on this—but even short songs have more than two verses, usually, don't they? And a chorus?

Keep going!
Mr. V

Jonny and I met again at lunchtime. We passed the activities board in the hall, and I spotted my sign, now hanging at a funky angle. It was starting to get tattered around the edges, and someone had written "LOSER" at the bottom!

That insightful comment had been there for at least three hours.

"This is so depressing," I said. Although it was probably time to pull the sign anyway—I hadn't gotten a single response after the ADHDisaster. I ripped the sign off, folded it up, and threw it in the trash.

"Ah, don't worry about it," Jonny said. "Child's play."

"What do you mean? That's so obnoxious."

"Sticks and stones, Cabrera. Forget about it. Listen, I've got a lead on a musician. A piano player."

"A *piano* player?" I hadn't really thought about keyboards—guitar, bass, and drums were the real essentials. I didn't want to sound too much like Benny and Joon, either.

"A *keyboardist*. Whatever. She can play."

"Well, okay. Sure." *Rule number one*, I thought. *Got to go for it.*

At this point, I probably would have hired a kazoo player if that kazoo player had shown some serious commitment. If I had to mold the talent, I'd mold the talent. Jonny said he had heard really good things about this girl, at least musically. He didn't say a *word* about her personality.

We walked down the hall and I spotted Bumblebee Shoes, the kid who was constantly being thrashed by the team of Federal Hill thugs. I gave him a nod. He started to give me a smile, but then he took a quick look at Jonny and turned white. The kid was so spooked, I guess anybody over five foot six gave him the heebie-jeebies.

"Did you see that?" I asked Jonny.

"What?" he said.

"Nothing." It was too complicated to explain.

Jonny led me up two flights of stairs to a short hallway on the top floor of the school.

"This is where the practice room is," Jonny said. "Every once in a while a band will work up here, but it's usually where the classical kids come to geek out and practice for an hour."

"I hear somebody going at it right now," I said. I could hear fast, furious classical piano music.

"Yup."

We peeked into the room and saw a girl absolutely punishing a piano. She stared at her sheet music like a psychic looking into a crystal ball, and she pounded the keys as if fighting some private war. The girl didn't notice us. Then the music changed, and suddenly she was playing quiet, spacey melodies. She looked like she was in a trance.

"Ah, yes. Crackers 'n' Cheese has some crazy technique," said Jonny.

"Crackers 'n' Cheese?" I repeated, loudly and stupidly. The music stopped.

"I don't like to be called that anymore," the girl said. She stood up so suddenly that the piano bench fell over. Furrowing her brow, she picked up the bench and then turned around to see who had so rudely interrupted her practice session. She was African American, very tall, beanpole thin, and had a goofy expression, like Martians had dropped her off on Earth, hightailed it back to space, then left her here to fend for herself.

"Wow, you're really tall!" I said. Duh. Another brilliant comment.

"Yep, I know." The girl popped a Triscuit in her mouth and followed it with a cube of orange cheese. Her lavender top was covered with crumbs.

"You've, uh, got something on your shirt," Jonny said, then, to me, explained, "That's why they call her Crackers 'n'—"

"It's just a snack," Crackers 'n' Cheese said, brushing off some crumbs.

"Hey, aren't you in Mr. V's class?" I asked.

"Yep."

"I thought you looked familiar."

"You look familiar, too, Annabelle Cabrera."

"How'd you know my name?"

"You talk a lot. You're kind of loud."

Loud? I had barely opened my mouth in that class.

"Well, what was that excellent music you were playing?"

"It's by the composer Ravel."

"Ra-who?" I said.

"Maurice Ravel. He's French."

"It's great. Play some more, Cracker— Sorry, what's your real name?" Jonny said.

"Christine. Christine Briar."

She put her hands on the keyboard again. At first, she didn't play a note. Resting her fingers on the keys, she closed her eyes and took one deep breath, then another. Jonny looked at me and raised an eyebrow. Then Crackers/Christine's hands started to move, and waves of big, round sound came out of the piano. With slim, powerful hands, she played up and down the instrument, her fingers racing across the keys like spiders. When she frowned, a big wrinkle appeared in the middle of her forehead, like there was an old woman trapped in her sixth grader's body.

"Whoa, that's amazing playing, Crackers," I said. "I mean, Christine. Want to join our band?"

"*Our* band?" Jonny said.

"Sorry, my bad," I said. "*My* band."

I explained the idea of the rock band while Crackers pigged out. How'd she get all those Triscuits into that skinny frame?

"You want to have a piano in your rock band?" Crackers asked.

"It might be kind of hard lugging a piano around to clubs, but I have a keyboard you can borrow. I want great musicians in my band, and you're pretty great."

"Well, I don't know if I'll ever be a *great* musician, but I definitely work at it."

Crackers started up the Ra-who piece again, playing even harder and faster while Jonny and I listened in awe. Crackers finished the piece with a flourish, closed the lid of the piano, and turned to us.

"I've thought it over and decided I'd like to participate."

Jonny gave me a quick whoa-she-could-be-nuts look, but I was stoked. I clapped my hands together, let out an embarrassingly girly squeal, and jumped in the air.

"Cool!" I said. "A band member! One down, a couple to go. Can you get together to practice this Saturday at my place?"

"Sure."

"Excellent. Thank you so much, Cr— Oops, sorry."

"It's okay," Christine said. "You can call me Crackers once

in a while. Just don't do it in the halls. And leave off the ''n' cheese,' please."

☆

I returned from school, and yet again there was no party in honor of my coming home. My parents barely looked up from the soundboard, where supposedly they were in the final stages of mixing. But they'd been saying that for weeks. X wasn't there. My mom said Jake had taken him over to Don's, so apparently his violent outburst hadn't gotten him banned for life.

I found Ronaldo on IM.

Bassinyrface: so do u think everyone in a band has to be cool?

EggMtnRckr: what do you mean?

Bassinyrface: I mean, I found a girl today who's a pretty amazing musician. But she's kind of strange.

EggMtnRckr: Strange how? Funny looking?

Bassinyrface: No, more . . . funny acting.

EggMtnRckr: yeah?

Bassinyrface: Like, she eats constantly, and she's always got crumbs all over her shirt, and people call her Crackers n Cheese!

EggMtnRckr: no way, seriously?

Bassinyrface: word.

EggMtnRckr: Well first of all, image is definitely a big deal. People arent just listening to you. Theyre WATCHING you.

Bassinyrface: I know. That kinda freaks me out.

EggMtnRckr: like at SummerStage that time.

Bassinyrface: yeah, exactly!

EggMtnRckr: But you got over that. And you always had good stage presence.

Bassinyrface: Thanks . . . but does my whole band need to have that? Stage presence?

EggMtnRckr: Well it does help. But it's not everything. As long as at least you and one other person in the band have it, you'll be all right.

Bassinyrface: And do they need to dress all rock? Because Jonny kind of does, but this girl dresses like a super dork.

EggMtnRckr: Mmmm, well maybe THAT will be your image.

Bassinyrface: ?

EggMtnRckr: like, maybe NOT having an image is your image.

Bassinyrface: Not following you. At all.

EggMtnRckr: Here's what I mean. It's back to the "Be Yourself" thing. Some bands who have a really intense image look really cool, and other bands look like theyre trying way too hard. Animal Collective had their animal mask thing going for a while, but now they just get up and play in T-shirts and jeans. You know?

Bassinyrface: yep.

EggMtnRckr: And take somebody like Bono. He's got the crazy big sunglasses that he wears like all the time.

Bassinyrface: Seriously, ALL the time! Weird.

EggMtnRckr: But it fits somehow. He's a big, loud guy and he wears big, loud shades.

Bassinyrface: And he's saving the world. One child at a time.

EggMtnRckr: Heh.

Bassinyrface: But yeah, I do get it. So we just have to sort of figure out who we are as a band, ya?

EggMtnRckr: Right. Then the image stuff can come later. And it'll make sense.

Bassinyrface: Gotcha. Thx.

☆

"Hey, Abuela, it's me, Annabelle, again." Here I was, leaving another message. "I'm sure you're busy as usual, but can you give me a call sometime?"

Did I sound mean? I didn't want to sound mean. I just really wanted her to call me back!

I went for more of an upbeat tone: "Today I think I found the first member of my new band. Or I might have two band members, if this one boy would just get it together and join already.

"He's a little nerdy, and she's addicted to snack food. But they're cool." Sort of. Cool enough to want to be in a band, anyway.

"X is still acting weird and begging for attention. But I'm the only one who'll give any to him, and I've got my own stuff to worry about, too. I don't mean to make you feel guilty, but will you call us? We miss you, Abuela . . . Bye."

Sometimes rock stars just need to hear from their grandmothers.

SHAKY IN THE HOUSE

Friday morning, I woke up with Satomi's fret board pressed against my face, "Dear Prudence" blasting through the speakers of my Beatles radio alarm clock. I wiped the dried drool off with my shirtsleeve. Gross! I must have fallen asleep practicing again. I leaned back and slid Satomi onto my belly, closing my eyes again and playing the Paul McCartney bass line for a minute before gathering the strength to face the day. Then I opened my eyes and got up, bass still on. Satomi had dug four rusty railroad tracks into my cheek with her fat strings. I scrubbed my face with a washcloth until it stung, but I could still see one long, wormlike line where the E string had been.

I brushed my teeth, ran water through my hair, got dressed, and walked into the kitchen, still groggy. My parents were nowhere in sight. No surprise there—they had still been mixing when I passed out, so now they were probably sleeping it off. X walked in, rubbing his eyes and carrying a periwinkle blue clapping monkey. He seemed to be going backward in time. Soon he'd be sucking his thumb and wearing Transformers underpants again.

"What's up, dude?" I said.

"You missed a spot, Belle," he said. "Been slobbering in your sleep again?"

"Very funny. How's your grounding going?"

"Okay, I guess." He looked down at his untied shoe, but made no move to tie it. "I don't see what I did wrong, anyway."

"You threw a cymbal at Dad's shin. That's a serious weapon, dude."

"Yeah, I guess. But grounded for two weeks? Come on."

"Well, it's not like you were doing anything ungrounded that you can't do now. You don't have any friends yet."

"Well, I can't skate. Inside or out."

I put out cereal and juice for both of us. X just sloshed the milk around in his bowl, not eating a bite.

"Would you please eat, X?" I said. "Mom must have forgotten to set her alarm, because I've been up for fifteen minutes and I haven't heard a peep from her."

"She's supposed to drive me to school today. We need to get some stuff for my log cabin."

"Your log cabin?"

"I have to make a log cabin out of clay." What? That made zero sense.

"Okay, I'll go get them."

"Shake 'em up to wake 'em up." My brother, the poet.

I climbed the ladder to the loft, and heard radio talk show

sounds coming from my parents' alarm clock. That was strange, because my mom was a light sleeper. She *never* slept through that thing. Something was up.

The comforter was draped perfectly across the bed, and a blanket was folded neatly across the bottom. The pillows had even been fluffed. My parents hadn't been there all night! I called out to my mom and dad, but I already knew there was no way they could be in the apartment.

This was a new one. I'd been left alone with X for a few hours before, but not without at least knowing where my parents were. X and I needed to be at school in a half hour, our parents had completely bailed on us without leaving a note, and I had no clue where they were or why they had left. Great!

I pulled out my phone and dialed my parents' numbers, and both went straight to voice mail. I checked my mom's bedside drawer for loose change. Bingo! Nine quarters and a whole bunch of nickels and dimes. I totaled it up and put the change—over four dollars' worth—in my pocket. That was enough for bus fare for both of us. If we left right now, I could drop X off at his school and probably still make it for half of Mr. V's class. I shimmied down the ladder, my heart thumping against my chest, telling myself to stay calm.

It made me realize I had almost never been alone before, truly alone. Even though my parents had spent most of their time away from the Sunset Park apartment, Abuela had always been there. It felt scary, but kind of exciting, too. I could already do just about everything on my own, anyway, and now I actually *was* on my own, independent, a grown-up.

"X, we're on our own today, okay?"

"What about my log cabin?"

"I don't know, buddy. I can't help you with that right now. The best I can do is get you to school on time."

"But it's supposed to be done already. Mom and Jake said they'd help me with it last night."

"Well, Mom or Jake can help you after school. But for now, we've both got to get going, okay?"

"I'm not even finished with my cereal."

"X! I just don't want to be late, okay?"

"Okay, okay," he said, but he wasn't really paying attention. He was looking over my head, toward the couch on the edge of the studio area.

"The couch just moved," he said. I heard a rustling sound and turned around.

"Belle? X?" said a sleepy voice. Shaky Jake, emerging from under a blanket on the studio sofa.

"Right here!" I said. I exhaled. Of course, Jake. "What happened? Where is everybody? How could they leave us alone like that?"

I ran over and gave him a slap on the shoulder, a *hard* one. I'm not sure what had gotten into me—it wasn't Jake's fault.

"Oof, watch it with the slapping, kid. Your parents have only been gone for a few hours." He rubbed his eyes and scratched his stomach through his long-underwear shirt. "And I've been here the whole time. Promise. Your dad was really excited about the recording, and he wanted to bring it straight to the mastering studio to finish up for real. He wants it online like immediately, so he was kind of jumping off the walls."

"Well, what about Mom? She was supposed to drive X to school and get him stuff for his project."

"Your dad really wanted her there with him. She said *I* should take X."

"Okay, whatever," I said. "X, I'll see you tonight."

I couldn't believe this. Now my parents weren't even spending the *nights* in the same apartment as us? Everything was turned upside down. I got my books and went out to catch the bus.

☆

Something oddly familiar about Mr. V had been bugging me from day one, and in class later that day, it finally came to me: Mr. V looked *exactly* like E.T. He probably wasn't older than forty-five, but his brown face was as crinkly as Abuela's. Walnut crinkly. He looked like a shrinkled old baby, and his fingers were so long they must have had an extra joint in them. Anyway, he liked my haikus, sort of.

> Forced Family Fun
> Drove us all bonkers today
> Ice cream, salty tears

> My dad loves music
> My mom loves what my dad does
> Where do kids fit in?

> It seems clear to me
> X chucked a cymbal at Dad!
> He just needs some love

I need this rock band
To keep from going crazy
When will it happen?

Ms. Cabrera,
Good work! You are mining your family life for
material, searching for universal truths.

What's so universal about my brother giving my father
a bloody shin? That's more like the universe spinning into
chaos.

But what exactly is this piece? Another song?
The rare extended-haiku form? I'm still not
getting the sense that this is a finished work, so
please keep going with it. You have given me a
couple of first drafts, but I want to see second
drafts, third drafts. Give me some polished work!

Christine whispered from the desk behind me. "You
wanna hang out at lunch?"

"Yeah, sure." I nodded. "I just need to grab a sandwich. I'll
meet you in the hall."

☆

On my way there, I saw another little kid crying in front of
his locker. He had to be the tiniest kid in the school, even
smaller than Bumblebee Shoes. His little-kidness was magni-
fied by the fact that he wore his hair in a bowl cut. That should
not be allowed after kindergarten under any circumstances,

but I guess this kid hadn't gotten the memo and let his mom do it anyway. He was slumped down with his head in his hands, crying so quietly that no one in the crowd of kids rushing to the cafeteria seemed to notice him. I tapped him on the shoulder.

"You okay?" I asked.

He didn't say anything, but he glanced up for a split second, and it looked like he had the beginnings of a nasty black eye. Somebody had socked him good.

"Who did it?" I asked. "A big curly-haired guy?"

"No." He sniffled. "The fat guy." Ouch. Didn't sound like Curly Burly.

"You need anything?" I asked.

"Well, I could use some lunch," he said. "They took all my money."

"Here," a voice said. I turned around, and it was Bumblebee Shoes. He handed the kid a sandwich, nodded to me, and said, "Thanks, I'll take it from here."

I got my own sandwich, then met Christine at her locker.

"You ever had somebody take your lunch money or threaten to beat you up?" I asked.

"No, but I've heard about it. That's why I started bringing my own." She pulled out a Ziploc and started chowing. "They just want cash, not Wheat Thins and pepper jack."

"They really walloped a kid I just saw. His eye's gonna be black and blue for a week."

"That's just the way things work around here," she said with her mouth full. "Let's go up to the practice room."

"I didn't bring my bass today."

"That's okay. Play your bass lines on the piano. We'll find *something* to work on."

I wasn't sure where Jonny was. Sick at home, maybe? This was the first time Christine and I had been alone together. She was all business. All about the music. I liked it.

"How long have you been playing the piano?"

"Since I was three."

"Three?!"

"My mom's a music teacher. I never really had a choice."

"But you like it, though, right?"

"Sure."

By the time we had climbed the stairs, I could hear some noise coming from the practice room. It wasn't music; it was the sound of a band just setting up: buzzing guitar amplifiers, rattling drumsticks, and sizzling cymbals. A sandpaper voice said "check, check" into a microphone. I gave Crackers the *shh* sign, and we peeked into the room.

"Okay, gentlemen, can we look alive, please?" said the voice.

"It's Raising Cain," Christine said. "They're about to start a song." The voice, so low it seemed to make the ground shake, belonged to Jackson Royer, the creep from the yard. We leaned against the doorjamb, safely out of view.

"Matt, tighten up your bass line on the verses," Jackson said. "And Darren, I want those snare hits on the chorus to be flams. We've got two trophies to defend, gentlemen. Show some pride." I could almost see him snickering. He didn't seem to really *mean* a single thing he said, and yet every sentence he uttered was a step away from a threat.

The room went quiet for an instant. Then the drummer

counted four fast beats with his sticks, and Raising Cain pounded out a blistering version of "Search and Destroy," an old Stooges song. Jackson growled out the first verse.

I have to admit, Raising Cain seemed to have mastered the Rules to Rock By. Jackson's guitar scraped and scratched like glass against the sidewalk. The bass was a deep, evil rumble. And each crack of the snare drum sounded like the deafening pop of a firecracker. But the band's power was in the way all the parts came together. Raising Cain was a single unit, strong and sleek, a wild beast about to bust out of its cage.

I couldn't help it. I had to have a better look. I stuck my head all the way inside. Jackson stood in the center of the room, his back to the door. He was wearing a sleeveless black T-shirt with the band's named etched in Gothic lettering. Original? No. But intimidating nonetheless.

Jackson stood with his legs spread wide and aligned under his shoulders. He slung his black Flying V guitar all the way down to his knees and barked into the microphone with a focused, controlled rage.

Then Jackson stopped suddenly and flashed the time-out sign to the band.

"Matty, I know you love your Heavy Metal pedal, but didn't we agree that you'd wait until the second verse?"

The kid looked at him blankly.

"Please nod your head. This is what is called an affirmation." Jackson used big words, like a public radio DJ or a major nerd. But the way he spoke them gave a completely different feeling. He sounded angry, but very, very controlled, making sure to keep the anger just underneath the words. "It indicates that we've had this conversation seventeen times and that while you've momentarily forgotten, you intend in the future to do as I say."

The bassist just nodded dumbly.

"Good boy . . . okay, let's start this thing up in a— What's that?"

It was my cell phone! I pulled it out as fast as I could— Abuela had chosen this moment of all the moments in the world to call me back—but by the time I had silenced it, it was too late. We were busted.

Jackson turned around calmly, grinning with satisfaction.

"Well, if it isn't Crackers 'n' Cheese and Beatles Girl. If I'm not mistaken, we're holding groupie auditions *tomorrow*, right, Darren? So what brings you two here today?"

I opened my mouth to speak, but all that came out were a few broken syllables.

"We were just coming up to use the piano. We didn't know you were here," Christine mumbled, almost inaudibly.

"Umm, sorry, Crackers von Crackerton, I must be hard of hearing. Were those words coming out of your piehole?" He turned to the drummer. "The child's mouth moves, yet I hear no sound." Laughter from the goons.

"Hey, Jackson, we have just as much of a right to this room as you guys do. Actually, we have more of a right." This time, Christine spoke loudly—I was surprised she had it in her—and pointed to the sign-up sheet on the wall. "See, that's my name. I had a reservation from twelve thirty to one."

"Oh my, an oversight," he mock-whimpered. "But what are the consequences? Is Principal Michaels personally going to eject us? Or perhaps the fetching new Spanish teacher? No? No one outside with a court order or a battering ram?"

Okay, so he was daring us to go tattle on him. I'd seen his type before, and that was not a challenge I was going to take him up on. I kept my silent-as-a-mime routine going, feeling powerless, like a complete idiot. And Christine's moment of courage seemed to have passed.

I looked around the room. The bass player was playing an Eastern-sounding scale up and down his fret board. He was probably bored by this stuff, had seen it a thousand times. But I recognized the drummer: it was Curly Burly, looking straight at me with those heavy-lidded eyes. He twirled a drumstick up in the air, then pointed it straight at me.

"I know you," he said. "You're the one from the hall. You're the one—"

"Darren, you're acquainted with Beatles Girl?" Jackson said.

Curly Burly's name was Darren? How could a dude that tough-looking, with the wallet chain and the heavy metal duds, be named *Darren*?

Jackson sat down on his amp and crossed his legs. "This chance meeting will be a happy reunion, I trust. How did you meet?"

"She made eye contact," Darren said. "First day of school. She—"

"Darren, you need to learn how to express yourself in— Far. Fewer. Words. Work on it, please." Jackson squinted and rubbed his chin. He strolled over until he was standing right in front of me, looking me over like a piece of merchandise he had decided wasn't worth legal tender. "Check out the trembling lip on Beatles Girl. She really does look terrified. You've done your job well, motormouth."

"Aye, aye, Captain."

"Well, shall we crank it back up, then?" Jackson signaled Darren, who ripped off a pounding drum fill. Jackson and the bassist dug into their strings, and Raising Cain resumed its merciless attack. Christine and I looked at each other in disbelief.

"What was he talking about?" she said.

I just shook my head. I still didn't have my words back. It was like one of those bad dreams where you're trying to yell or scream but the sound just won't come out. I touched my face. My lower lip was definitely not trembling! I was a little nervous; that was all. Okay, more than nervous. Freaked out. Slightly humiliated. But mostly, just really annoyed!

Another Annabelle rule:

Rock stars are not intimidated by rival bands.

TURKEY MEATBALLS

When I came home, Ronaldo popped up on IM.

EggMtnRckr: wassup Belle?
Bassinyrface: hey, R.
EggMtnRckr: I read your email. He seriously said EYE CONTACT? Like he doesnt let anybody look him in the eye? I guess he thinks he's Prince William or something, and not the loser leader of a middle school cover band.
Bassinyrface: ☺
EggMtnRckr: Listen, just stay out of his way. Lay low.
Bassinyrface: I know, but there's something about this guy that just makes me want to . . . I dunno.
EggMtnRckr: what?

Bassinyrface: Make him stop being so full of himself. And mean.

EggMtnRckr: No matter what you do, u cant change that about him. Trust me!

Bassinyrface: More wisdom from the professor, eh?

EggMtnRckr: you know it.

Bassinyrface: YOU are a know-it-ALL sometimes, you know that?

EggMtnRckr: Maybe. Just trying to help! I've had my share of that kind of guy before. U don't think I've gotten guys like that messing with me? with how I dress?

Bassinyrface: I know, it's true. You have more bully experience than me.

EggMtnRckr: I'm not saying run away. I'm just saying keep a low profile, girl! Is that so hard?

Bassinyrface: no.

EggMtnRckr: Actually, I know you! Staying mellow is gonna be almost impossible for you, huh?

Bassinyrface: Heh. Maybe. We'll see . . .

☆

"Come here buddy, I got a message from Abuela today. You wanna listen to it?"

X skated over to my bed and sat next to me.

"Doesn't that violate your grounding, little man?" I asked. "Skating in the house?"

"Not if you don't tell Mom and Dad about it," he said.

"Good point. Mum's the word. Unless you mess with me, that is."

I set the phone to speaker and started the message.

"Annabella and Chabito"—this was her special nickname for X—"this is your Abuela, your grandmama, calling you to say hello. Annabelle, I sorry I do not call you before. Things very busy, and the recorder no work no more. Consuela she giving me the message but it's gonna be too late.

"I miss you. I miss our family like it once was. And I know you do also. But things will be good. They will be better. I promise you, okay?"

Abuela paused, and I thought I could hear the scratchy rasp of one of her old lady friends in the background, probably barking at the TV.

"This is what you need to do, okay, *mis angeles*? Don't do a lot of things wrong for you fathers. And you need to try to make the family happy, make the family proud, always be good boy and good girl. Be beautiful, and then the world, it will be beautiful for you, too. Okay? *Besos, besos.*" Abuela's smacking kissy sounds. "And Chabito . . . he can hear me, Annabelle? Chabito, you try to live more normal for me, okay?"

X shrugged as I closed the phone.

"Normal, shnormal," X said.

"Whatever, Trevor," I said, sighing. Why couldn't she have moved here with us? She said she was too old to move anywhere at her age, that she would have to literally be dragged out of her apartment when she died. I couldn't even think about that. All I knew was that, without her, we were falling apart.

☆

That night, Mom put on a big show of making dinner for the whole family, including Shaky Jake. I could smell the good-food-cooking smells from my room/personal area. I could hear the sounds of pots and pans clanging, and instantly I knew exactly what was going on: she was trying to win our hearts back through our stomachs.

Making turkey meatballs was one of the only actual momlike things Mom ever did, and back in Brooklyn I used to feel lucky if it happened once every couple of months. Abuela was the cook of the family, and Mom knew how to prepare two, maybe three dishes. So if Mom was cooking, it was usually to make a point: that a woman who had once been called the "ice princess of indie rock" by *Blender* magazine could also roll up her sleeves and transform herself into a regular stay-at-home type—or, as in this case, to make up for something horribly irresponsible that she had done earlier that day.

I sat at the edge of the kitchen and watched her, dirty blond hair in a ponytail, furiously chopping onions and mixing them into a big ball of goodness in the mixing bowl. She shaped the mixture into tight, rounded balls and began to cook them to a delicious golden brown. It was a smart strategy. One whiff of the air in that kitchen was enough to make me swoon.

But would I let her get away with this? Let her buy my forgiveness through my taste buds? Perform emotional bribery with oregano and bread crumbs? No way. It wasn't going to work this time. Parents couldn't just bail on their kids in the middle of the night, recording or no recording. And they couldn't make up for it with one meal, however yummy.

It was my goal to say no more than ten words during the whole dinner.

"Someday I'd like to mix our whole catalog in surround sound," Dad was saying as we all sat down.

"Interesting," was Jake's reply, although he didn't actually sound that interested.

Dad was in outer space. I knew that, and I didn't have the unrealistic expectation that he would feel bad about what he had done. Bigger storms had come and gone without him noticing a cloud in the sky. Mr. V said the other day that the definition of insanity is doing or seeing the same thing over and over again and expecting a different result. No matter how many times I heard Dad obsess about music over the dinner table while barely nodding hello to his own children, I hoped things would be different. But they never were. So I guess that made me crazy.

I decided to concentrate all my silent fury on my mom. She was clueless, but not as clueless as my dad. She wasn't too clueless to be made to feel guilty. I wanted her to feel *bad*, and for a good long while.

"So, how was school?" Mom asked, taking off her apron. She wore a sheer periwinkle shirt. The short sleeves had pretty frills at the ends, and tiny white butterflies decorated the fabric.

"Fine." I sat down at the table, not meeting her eyes. *One word. One out of ten.* X sat across from me with his clapping monkey.

I twirled pasta around my fork, making sure my expression wasn't sad or angry. I just went for emptiness, wide-open emptiness that would keep Mom guessing. I was good at this.

X was inhaling his pasta and making rhymes about his

two favorite foods, orange sherbet and Dr. Brown's Cel-Ray soda. These two items had been mostly off-limits in Brooklyn, when Abuela was in charge of the shopping and cooking. Abuela used to let X have orange sherbet on holidays and other special occasions, and once a month or so she'd go all the way to a Lower East Side deli to buy a six-pack of Cel-Ray, a soda that actually mixed in celery flavor along with the regular five pounds of sugar. Back then, these things had been only once-in-a-while treats. Now X wanted them every day. My mom had pretty much caved in when it came to the orange sherbet, letting X have some every night after dinner. But she couldn't find Cel-Ray anywhere.

"Sunday, Monday, X wants a Cel-Ray," X chanted. "Tuesday, Wednesday, I know my mom'll find a way!"

Mom succeeded in calming Xavier down after a while by squeezing a lime into his ginger ale and giving him her most serious enough-is-enough stare. Then she got even more ambitious, trying to get *me* to talk again, to answer questions with more than one-syllable answers. She admitted that going to the mastering studio had been "bad judgment" and that she'd start being "more aware of" X's and my "needs." She tried to puncture my armor with these measly peace offerings. But it wasn't going to work, and she knew it. She shifted tactics.

"Are you still enjoying that English class you said you liked? The one with the funny teacher?"

"It's fine." *Three.*

"Have you been looking for bandmates?"

"No." *Four.*

"Have you made any other friends?"

"Nope." That made five words that I'd spoken since dinner had started. Mom put her fork down and leaned over, trying to get me to make eye contact. I gave her a glance that lasted less than a half second.

"Belle, not all your friends need to be musicians, you know. I'll bet there are all kinds of neat kids at Federal Hill."

Neat kids?

"Whatever, Mom." *Seven.* Bad move. She couldn't offer me advice and parental wisdom on the same day she had abandoned me in the middle of the night.

"Belle's never been great at making friends," said my dad, as if I weren't sitting right there in front of him. "She's a loner, like me, dreaming about music."

Then he turned to me. "Annabelle, I love the way you've taken after me with your music. It's something that'll stay with you for the rest of your life. But you need to work on making friends, too, and keeping them. Maybe you need to . . . I don't know, soften your edges a little bit?"

"What are you talking about? I don't have any edges!" Enraged at the fact that my dad had made me go over my word count by seven, I picked up my plate and headed toward the sink. But now that my plan had been shot to pieces, I couldn't resist coming back to the table to stir things up a little. I guess I hadn't fully mastered the art of sulking.

"So, Dad, how'd your *masterpiece album* turn out? Was it worth it?"

"Well, I don't know if it's a masterpiece, but—"

"Really? Then why bother? What's the point if it's not going to be your *Sgt. Pepper's,* your *Doolittle,* your *OK Computer?*"

"I don't know what you're getting at, Belle, but I'm quite sure I don't like your tone."

Both my parents pulled this trick. Ninety-nine percent of the time they didn't act the least bit like parents, but as soon as they didn't like the way I was acting, they came out with all the things they thought parents were *supposed* to say: "I'm not sure if I like your tone," "Watch yourself, young lady," "You've got an attitude problem," etc.

"Okay, how about this tone? Do you agree with all the bloggers that say you guys haven't made a good record since *Entranced*?" Even X looked up from his state of orange-sherbet gluttony to see the response to that one.

"That's enough, Belle," said my mom. "Go to your room. This instant!"

She didn't even sound like a real parent. She sounded like a fake mother in a black-and-white movie, an actor reading from a script.

"I don't even *have* a room! My room is four walls away from being a room! It's just a *personal area!*"

"Well, go to your *personal area*, then!" Mom said. "Right now!"

I ran into the kitchen and paced back and forth in front of the sink. I was stomping so hard that my feet actually ached, and the room seemed to be moving, not me. Everything was a blur, and my brain felt hot with anger. Then I reached into the sink, grabbed the plate I had just put there, and smashed it to the floor.

"Belle!" my mom shouted as I ran to my room, to my area, to whatever it was, cursing the fact that it didn't even have a door I could slam. I just jumped on my bed and put the pillow over my head. I tried to calm myself down by going through Beatles lyrics in my head, but it didn't work. How could my parents be that clueless? How could they treat X and me like we were just another piece of baggage they had to take up north with them to make their home-studio dream come true?

I needed a real band more than ever now. Anything to take me away from all this. A band would be my magic carpet, my escape route out of this stupid situation.

"Belle?" It was my mom. "I'm sorry, honey."

"Go away!"

"Can we talk? Please?"

"I don't feel like it."

"Jake is here. Will you talk to him?"

"No!"

That took the cake. Things had gotten so bad with my parents, they had forgotten how to even *be* parents. They needed a big bearded drummer to raise their own kids.

I waited until I was sure they had both walked away and weren't coming back, opened up my notebook, and wrote:

> You stand there trying to say the right
>   things
> But I can't even look you in the eye
> When you wake up, see I've left this place
> Will you even cry?
>
> I wonder, will it hurt you bad?
> When I turn from you and run?

I'll be the one with the last word
Heading for the setting sun

I titled it "Setting Sun." As they say in the business, this song-to-be "wrote itself." If my parents were going to drive me insane, maybe I could at least get some lyrics out of it.

Rock stars use their lame family lives as material for songs.

THE FIRST PRACTICE

"Abuela, I *know* you want me and X to do what Mom and Dad say," I said to Abuela bright and early the next morning, a Saturday. "But I don't think you're really getting the situation."

Abuela had woken me up with a phone call at the ungodly hour of 7:13 a.m. and had just finished her "make your fathers proud" speech.

"How you mean, Annabella?" she said.

"What I mean is that I can't make them 'proud' if they're never even around."

"They really spending so much time outside of house?"

"Yes, Abuela, they really are. But what's worse is how they never notice what's going on with us. I mean, X is not the same as when you last saw him. He's so hyper and crazy, going bonkers constantly."

"This is no good. No good."

"And Mom and Dad haven't met any of my teachers yet, or anything. I probably hang out more with my English teacher than I do with them."

"*Mi angelita,* I did not know this. I so sorry. This also no good."

"And Jake makes us chocolate chip pancakes like four times a week. Last night, Mom made turkey meatballs. That's the first real sit-down meal we've had as a family in Providence. And it ended in a fight."

"What?!?!" She screeched so loudly I had to pull my ear away from the phone. "You eating pancakes? For dinner? Annabella, this is very, very, very bad. Why you no tell me this before? Shaking Jake no can cook for *my* family. That red-beard man no cook for *my* grandchildrens. I gonna talk to your fathers now. For sure! Nobody making the good food for you? I very upset about this, my baby. I no happy at all."

☆

"How you doin', Belle?" the red-beard man asked me only moments after I hung up the phone with Abuela.

But I didn't want to talk about it. "I'm having a band practice. With only one measly bandmate! I need at least one more musician, Jake. Otherwise we'll be a joke!"

I had just finished cleaning up the broken dish that my parents had left from the night before with a note from my dad next to it saying, "You broke it, you clean it up." I could hear my parents stirring upstairs, and I was trying to finish this chat with Jake before they came down.

Jake had a homemade carrot cake in the oven and was licking some of the leftover batter off a spatula. The light orange color matched his beard and head hair perfectly. "Want some?" he asked, and I shook my head. In Brooklyn, Abuela had absolutely forbidden him to make his cakes after the time he'd clogged her drain with carrot peels and she'd had to call a plumber.

"How did you hook up with the bands you've been in, Jake?"

"Well, drummers are in demand. Always. I've never really had to look for people to play with. They've found me."

"Well, all I know is that it's been two months and I'm not even close to having a band. And every time I ask people about how they put theirs together, they make it sound like it just *happened*. Like magic."

"Well, it is kind of like that," said Jake. "You put yourself out there, and things just start to work for you."

"Well, I've *been* putting myself out there."

"It can take some time." He licked his fingers.

"Yeah, yeah."

"And listen, I'm psyched to jam with you if you need a drummer."

"Thanks, Jake. I'll keep you in mind. If I decide to form a band with senior citizens. Who drool." I pointed to the batter in his beard. "Seriously, though, this is something I want to do *on my own*. With kids *my age*."

"Yep, I get it. Oh, listen, just a quick word before your mom and dad get in here, okay? I think they're going to ask you to take care of your brother again today."

"Jake, when are they going to stop letting you do their dirty work for them?"

"They didn't ask me. I just wanted to give you . . . a little warning."

Just then, Mom walked in.

"Mom, I have to take care of X today? I have band practice."

"We're doing an unplugged thing on WBRU today," she said. "I told you."

"You did *not* tell me, Mom!"

"Listen, Annabelle, I know the timing isn't great. And I know you're having your friend over to play. You don't even have to watch X. He'll entertain himself. You know how he is."

"I know exactly how he is, Mom." I could hear Dad walking around up in their bedroom. He was probably waiting until this conversation was over to come down.

"It's not like I'm complaining because I don't like being with X. He's fine. Everybody loves him, blah, blah, blah. But why does it have to be *me* always taking care of him? Ever since we moved, it's like *I'm* the mom and you and Dad are just . . . not even around."

My mom looked like she'd been slapped in the face, and I thought, *Good. At least you're paying attention.*

"Look, the move's been hard on all of us," she said. "But we're going to get through it. We're going to get through this album, the shows, your new school, X's new school—all of it. But we all have to pitch in. And today I need you to help look after X for me. We'll be back in three hours. Okay?" She looked like she was about to give me a hug or a kiss or something, but then thought better of it, grabbed her bag, and headed for the door.

"We ready?" Dad said, climbing down the loft ladder.

"Yeah, we're ready, hon."

Jake took the carrot cake out of the oven and put it on the stove top to cool. It smelled delicious.

"For you and your bandmate, Belle," Jake said, and then pointed to a small mixing bowl on the counter. "Wait for it to cool, and then put this frosting on top."

"Thanks, Jake," I said.

And just like that, the three of them were out the door.

I barely looked up, stirring a spoon aimlessly in my empty cereal bowl. This was not the glorious first day of band practice I had imagined. I was basically going to be babysitting not one but two kids: my brother, a fourth grader who spoke in chants, and a classical music dork who would probably be shoving Wheat Thins and cheese slices down her throat all day long, leaving a trail of crumbs around the apartment like Hansel and Gretel. Some rock band.

X came into the kitchen. "Belle," he said. "Hang out with me."

For the next half hour, I was probably the least energetic Texas Hold'em partner X had ever faced. "Are you *awake*?" he kept saying. "You're just letting me win."

"No, I'm not," I said. "I seriously have no idea how this game works." It was true. If you ever want to put me to sleep, start explaining to me what the heck you're supposed to do in poker.

When the doorbell finally rang, I had practically forgotten Crackers 'n' Cheese was even coming. I slumped down the hall and hit the buzzer, barely caring.

"We're here," she said through the intercom.

"Come up to 5G," I said. *We're* here? That was definitely what Crackers had said. I opened the door and waited for the elevator to make its slow climb to the fifth floor.

"Surprise!" called out Crackers *and* Jonny.

"Jonny, what are you doing here?"

"I was afraid Christine would get lost," he said, grinning slyly. "I don't know about being in a band or anything, but I figured I could at least rock out with you guys a little." He turned around, revealing the guitar case strapped on his back. I tried to play it cool, but I was really excited and couldn't stop smiling for a full minute. Who knew how many of Ronaldo's rules I'd polish off today?

In the studio, we plugged in our instruments and a couple microphones and set up the drum set, even though no one, including me, had ever really played it. After that, we puttered around for a few minutes, straightening cords and checking amp levels. I don't know about those other guys, but I'm ready to admit that I was stalling. The big moment was here. I had a band! The beginnings of one, at least. It wasn't like me, but, yeah, I felt shy.

"Well, we could try this little riff I wrote," I said. I picked out the same White Stripes rip-off that had totally bowled over my dad on forced-family-fun day.

Christine stood and listened for a bit.

"Sounds like metal," she said. Metal? What did she know about metal? She might have known Ra-who, but my riff was not a metal riff.

"Sounds cool," Jonny said, and started playing along,

echoing the riff on the guitar. He stepped on a little metal box called a "flanger," which made his guitar sound like it was underwater. Then he stepped on another one, a Big Muff distortion pedal, and the riff went giant and fuzzy. Finally, Crackers figured out her part: a few spacey chords on my mom's Nord 2 keyboard. This instant-mix song sounded a little messy and odd at first, but after a few minutes something strange and beautiful started to happen. It really sounded like music. This "band" had its first "song."

I played around with some *ooohs* and *aaahs* before realizing that I might be able to mine my notebook for lyric ideas. I remembered my "Dumb Puppies" title idea from the first day of school and decided to play around with it:

Big dumb puppies
Foul my school.
Sad little dogs
Only know to play the fool.
Puppy, puppy,
Do as you're told!
Puppy, puppy,
Your act is getting old!

Okay, it wasn't a masterpiece exactly. These lyrics needed a *lot* of work. But it was something. It sounded like a song.

It felt really strange to sing in front of Jonny and Crackers. I hadn't expected to feel nervous—after all, I had sung in Central Park to literally thousands of people—but I did.

"You have such a sweet voice!" said Christine.

"It's true, it's nice, it's . . . not quite what I expected," said Jonny. "Pretty," he blurted awkwardly.

Sweet, huh? *Pretty?* Rock 'n' roll isn't *pretty*. I didn't want to sound pretty.

"Let's run through it one more time," I said. I sang the melody again, but with more attitude, more growl. I tried one of my full-length-mirror rock star poses, pointing the head-stock of the bass toward the ceiling.

"Belle, go back to being yourself," Jonny said. "It works."

"Yeah," said Christine.

Ouch. Did they think I was being a poser or something? I tried not to worry about it. If Jonny thought I could sing, that was enough for me. When Satomi sang, she sounded like a four-year-old child or a baby alien from Jupiter, and she was my hero. So maybe it was okay to sound "pretty," even if it wasn't very intimidating.

We kept working on the riff. In honor of Crackers's early review, we titled it "Belle's Metal Riff" and broke for lunch.

☆

"This is my little brother, guys," I said. "X, this is Jonny. And Crack— Christine."

"*Hola,* Jonny. What's up, Crack Christine?" he said, making himself a PB&J.

"Just Christine," I said, pouring out four Cokes.

"So, Annabelle, you know that place Don Daddio's?" Jonny asked.

"Ha, I sure do. X almost destroyed the place a few days ago."

"I *thought* I recognized you," Jonny said. "You're the kid who hangs in the percussion room."

"What's left of the percussion room," I said.

"That's me," X said, putting a plate with four PB&Js on the table.

"Thanks," I said. See, my brother could be cool. When it was just us, he was fine. It was only when my parents were around that he flipped out.

"Thanks," said Jonny and Christine.

"Anyway, what about Don's?" I asked.

"Well, I was in there picking up strings on the way over," Jonny said. "Have you seen this?"

He unfurled a flyer:

DON DADDIO PRESENTS
6TH ANNUAL
MINOR THREAT BATTLE OF THE KID BANDS
WHEN: FRIDAY, NOVEMBER 18, 5:30 P.M.
WHERE: DON'S
WHO: ANYBODY, AS LONG AS EVERYONE IN YOUR BAND IS AGE 18 OR YOUNGER
WHY: THE CHANCE TO ROCK YOUR FRIENDS' FACES OFF AND ACHIEVE ROCK 'N' ROLL GLORY, FAME, RENOWN, STARDOM, ETC.

PLUS: WINNER GETS OPENING SLOT AT BROWN UNIVERSITY'S SPRING FLING IN MAY!!!!!!

"Wow, cool. How could I not know about this?" I said, thinking, *Yes! Rule number five—our first gig—here we come!*

"What do you mean?" Jonny asked.

"I practically lived in that store over the summer. Don's like my uncle."

"Well, that's a coincidence, because Don really *is* my uncle." Jonny bit into his sandwich.

"Are you serious? You're so lucky."

X had already finished his meal, and Crackers joined him on the floor, ramming monster trucks into the cabinetry. A perfect match, those two.

"So, what about this battle of the bands?"

"Could be cool," I said. "But does that mean we're a band? Jonny Mack, Mr. Solo Career?"

"Well, no, it doesn't. I mean, I really don't want to be in a band. But I do want to help you."

"I don't get it."

"Well, I'll tell you what. I'll sub for you until you find a real guitarist. We can practice, record, whatever. But if you want to play live, it's got to be somebody else. You've got nine weeks till the battle. You'll find somebody before *then*."

"Okay, that works." I nodded. "So, what's Spring Fling anyway?"

"Well, it's basically just an excuse for all the kids at Brown to party before finals, but the lineup is always amazing. Vampire Weekend—"

"Not a fan."

"Hold your horses, Cabrera. Let me think . . . M.I.A. did it a couple years ago."

"Nice, now we're talking."

"Brian Jonestown Massacre, Deerhoof . . ."

I didn't say a thing. Didn't want to come off cocky. But I

couldn't stop thinking, what if I could open up for Satomi, again!

"Well, duh, it would be sweet to play with any of those bands," I said. "I guess I gotta find me a guitar player. And a drummer. But where?"

Where, indeed. Of all the instrumentalists, drummers were notoriously the hardest band members to find. I'd heard my dad say this over and over again, citing the number of dud drummers he'd worked with before he'd met Jake. The ones who could play, he'd said, had terrible personalities, and the ones he could stand to be in the same room with, well, they usually played too many notes, forgetting that they were playing in a *band*, not a drum solo recital. Yes, it was going to be tough, especially in a middle school, but now that I had a guitarist, or at least half a guitarist, I was starting to feel like maybe, just maybe, it was going to happen.

Rock stars dare to dream. (And they dare to write cheesy rock star rules.)

SERIOUS LUNGS

I found Ronaldo on IM the following Thursday morning, the first day of October. The windows were open, and I could already feel a chill in the air. Autumn was here.

Bassinyrface: so it looks like I might have the beginnings of a band, finally.
EggMtnRckr: yeah? Is Jonny in?
Bassinyrface: no, not yet. He's definitely playing with us but he says he doesnt want to actually be in the band.
EggMtnRckr: Hmmm . . . why's that?
Bassinyrface: yeah I dont know what his deal is.
EggMtnRckr: Is he as cool of a guy as he seemed like at first?

Bassinyrface: Yeah, definitely.

EggMtnRckr: Well, keep working on him. He'll come around.

Bassinyrface: Ok, thx. How are things in Egg Mtn world?

EggMtnRckr: problemas, mi amiga. looks like no more fast eddie for egg mtn.

Bassinyrface: what?!?

EggMtnRckr: he says he's outgrown the band. We're too soft for him!

Bassinyrface: sux!

EggMtnRckr: he says he wants to form a speed metal band!!!

Bassinyrface: Stupid! Although . . . I've got just the band for him. Only thing is, theyre in Providence!

EggMtnRckr: heh heh . . . those goons you told me about, eh? Razing Kane?

Bassinyrface: yep. you looking for another guitar player then?

EggMtnRckr: Yep, i guess we both are.

As I signed off that IM conversation, my whole body was tingling. I used to have those tingles, that pent-up feeling of excitement, on Christmas morning waiting to unwrap gifts. That made sense. Presents were exciting! But hearing that your former band had lost its most skilled musician? There was nothing thrilling about that, so why did I have happy goose bumps all over? I had no right to be excited about Ronaldo's bad luck. But in a strange, upside-down way, I was.

Maybe I was just glad that I wasn't the only band leader struggling to put it all together.

☆

The upside-down feeling continued all day. Just before first period, I was looking for Jonny. We were going to practice at his house after school, and I needed to find out how to get there. I turned a corner and saw him standing in front of his locker, but he was talking to some tall guy. The tall guy's back was turned to me, and Jonny was so concentrated on what the guy was saying that he didn't notice I was there. But something about the way the two stood together made me hesitate. They were talking quietly, but with a nervous energy I could sense from fifteen feet away. I ducked behind some lockers and watched. Actually, all the tension was coming from Jonny, who was visibly shaken up. The tall guy was completely relaxed, talking quickly but calmly and making his points with confident hand gestures. As he turned toward the left, I got a better view of his ugly mug: it was Jackson Royer. What could Jonny possibly have to talk about with Jackson Royer? Although, really, it looked pretty one-way as far as conversations go.

Jackson had only a couple of inches on Jonny height-wise, but the way he carried himself, he looked a lot bigger. Jackson had his arms folded, and Jonny seemed to slump in response. He looked like he didn't want anybody to see him; his bangs hung over his glasses and, as usual, he kept his eyes down, like he was bowing to Jackson the god. Could Jackson really be bullying a kid as big as Jonny? My first urge was to go over there and make some noise, defend my friend.

But something held me back. Fear, maybe, but it was more than that. I just had a feeling that if I interrupted them, something bad might happen.

Jackson leaned in farther, just inches away from Jonny, still speaking too quietly for me to hear. He poked Jonny in the sternum with his index finger. Jonny nodded, reached into his front pocket, and gave Jackson a big wad of bills and change. Jackson took it, looked around to make sure no one was watching, pocketed the wad, and was gone. I waited to make sure Jackson didn't turn around, then snuck off in the other direction.

☆

More upside-downness. As I walked to English I heard music blaring out of Mr. V's classroom. Rock music. The man had set up a giant pair of desktop speakers and was playing none other than Bon Jovi. As I sat down, everyone around me was pointing and giggling as Mr. V sat cross-legged on his desk, sandwiched by the speakers, which must have been cranked to eleven. The music was so loud I could barely think, but he wore his usual expression of Buddha-like calm.

"Students, today we have no blue bowl," Mr. V said, turning the speakers down, but just a little. "Today we will do something a little bit more interesting. Everyone likes music, am I correct?"

"Yeah, *good* music maybe, not this trash!" said that goon McNamara. More upside-downness—I actually agreed with the goons.

"Mr. McNamara, I will tolerate insults to Shakespeare, to Emerson, to Hemingway, but please lay off Jon Bon Jovi. Many of his songs are on the soundtrack of my life."

"What soundtrack of your life?" another goon asked.

"Thank you so much, Mr. Amado, for providing such a convenient segue. Pause a moment and listen to the words of Mr. Bon Jovi."

He turned up the speaker volume again, and the class was treated to some cheesy lyrics about how life is like a huge open road and how you could die any minute, so you need to go down that huge open road in a giant white Cadillac with the wind blowing your long wavy hair, and blah, blah, blah. There was also something about a guy named Frankie, but JBJ never explains who Frankie even is. Yawn.

"That's truly beautiful," said McNamara. But you could tell he meant the exact opposite. Maybe McNamara and I would be friends one day?

"Thank you. Now, students," he said, smiling and raising that left eyebrow of his. "Some of you might not care for this particular song. I happen to find it quite invigorating. And it would certainly be on the soundtrack of my life. It was playing the first time I saw the woman who would become my wife.

"I want all of you to think about the songs that would be on *your* soundtrack. Take these."

He passed a handout around:

The Soundtrack of My Life, Part One
Instructions: Songs are the poetry of our everyday lives.
Find some poetry in your life by choosing your soundtrack.
Many songs have a meaning, or a message. But some
songs are just fun and enjoyable. Don't think too hard.
The thinking will come in parts two and three. For now,
just look at the categories below and choose a beloved

song that fits it. Start hunting while also making sure that your choices are of a *school-appropriate nature*!

1. Opening Credits
2. Receiving a Gift
3. Treasured Memory
4. Disagreement
5. Making Up
6. Moment of Regret
7. The Happy Dance
8. Loneliness
9. The Final Battle
10. Closing Credits

Sometimes, I swear Mr. V was talking directly to me. I spent the rest of the class madly scribbling at least three possibilities per category, and I decided to forgive Mr. V for saying he loved Bon Jovi. He was still my favorite teacher.

Good teachers are allowed to have questionable taste in rock stars.

☆

On my way back to my locker, I saw Jackson again. The guy was unavoidable. For probably the millionth time, he was roughing up Bumblebee Shoes just outside the boys' bathroom. Jackson was leaning into him and poking him in the chest.

"I think it's wonderful that you've started to bring your lunch to school," Jackson said. "What have you got there? Turkey sand? Apple? What else? Ooh, the old standby, a Fruit Roll-Up. Kid, this is a healthy alternative to the garbage they sell at the caff, but I'm afraid it doesn't alter our . . . financial agreement in the slightest. Cough up the cash."

Bumblebee Shoes did cough, literally, as he handed him some loose change. "It's all I've got," he said. "My mom doesn't give me lunch money anymore."

Jackson caught me looking. After seeing him mess with Jonny, I guess I just didn't care anymore.

"Hello, Beatles Girl."

"Leave him alone, Jackson," I said.

"What did you say?" Jackson asked.

"I'm not afraid of you." I seriously have no idea why I chose to say that when it was so obviously untrue. My lower lip was trembling all over the place.

He let go of Bumblebee Shoes and took two steps toward me. "Yes, you are."

I took three steps back. "You can't just take his money." And how was I going to stop him? I hadn't thought that part through just yet.

"Take his money? I'm not taking his money. He gives it of his own free will. If you're suggesting that I have threatened this young man with physical injury if he doesn't comply with my wishes, I resent the accusation." He turned to Bumblebee Shoes. "Young man, have I threatened you in any fashion?"

The kid only looked at him questioningly.

"Have I physically harmed you, or hinted that I might do so?"

"Uh, no?"

"You see, Beatles Girl? We don't threaten. We converse. We persuade. We reach agreements. Now skedaddle to class so that my friend and I can continue our chat."

I looked around. No teachers, no civilians, no two-hundred-pound weight-lifter buddies. I had no choice. I skedaddled.

☆

Jonny was throwing a lot of curve balls my way. Not only did he seem to have some strange connection to Jackson, but he had also offered up his house for practice. I didn't get it—if he wasn't really "in the band," then why was he getting so involved? But it was fine with me. He had an extra amp and keyboard we could use, so all I needed was my bass, and Christine didn't have to bring a thing. Lately the last place I wanted to be was my own house anyway. The whole apartment was still shaking with the aftershocks of X's cymbalic violence and my turkey meatball explosion. I was happy for a change of scenery.

And it was a *major* change. Jonny's neighborhood was across the interstate from Federal Hill, on the East Side. We lived on the East Side, too, but not on College Hill, where Jonny's family lived. We had to take a different bus to his place. When it pulled up, he and Crackers and I got on. We quickly sped through Federal Hill, then to downtown's big bank-type buildings.

"If you live all the way up there, why do you go to Federal Hill?" I asked.

Jonny just shrugged.

When we climbed up Memorial Boulevard, the neighborhood changed completely. Unlike the warehouses that packed my non-neighborhood, or the simple homes near school, the giant brick buildings of Brown University and the Rhode Island School of Design were classy and pretty. Christine gave me a look, like, *Wow, fancy.* I had been on Thayer Street a bunch of times, which runs right through Brown, but I had never come up the hill from this angle. As the bus turned off Waterman Street, it wound around wide blocks with tall trees that looked like they were hundreds of years old. By the time we got out, we were on what was probably one of the most beautiful streets in Providence.

"This is nice," Crackers said. "*Really* nice."

I didn't want to make a big deal out of it, but I was thinking the same thing: *Is Jonny rich? Is that why he handed over that big wad of cash to Jackson?*

The trees had turned about a week earlier; rust- and orange-colored leaves shimmered in the afternoon light. And the houses were big and beautiful, with porches and front *and* back yards. We didn't have setups like this in Brooklyn, or even Manhattan. You could be the richest person in all of New York City and still not have a big front yard with perfect grass.

"What do your parents do?" Crackers asked Jonny. Was that rude? I was glad she had asked, though, because I was curious, too.

"My dad's in the history department at Brown, and my mom's at RISD. She's an associate professor of illustration."

"What's that?" Crackers asked.

"She teaches drawing, basically."

"You can live in a neighborhood like this teaching drawing?"

"Yeah, I guess." He looked down, like he was trying to avoid the subject.

"Are those Ionic, Doric, or Corinthian?" I asked, pointing out the three giant columns on what I figured was Jonny's front porch.

"I have no idea," he said.

"Look Doric to me," I said. I had had to memorize that stuff in fifth grade. Doric were the simple ones, Ionic had small curlicues at the top, and Corinthian were super fancy, over-the-top.

"Definitely Doric," Crackers said.

"Oh, but that's not my house. That's the Havemeyers' house. They're our landlords."

"Oh," I said.

Jonny led us through the side yard of the fancy house to the backyard. Just to the left stood a little yellow wooden house. It was two floors, but it was barely bigger than our apartment. *So then where did he get all that money?* I wondered.

"This is where the servants used to live back in the day," Jonny said.

"Yeah, but your parents aren't servants, they're professors," I said.

"*Associate* professors," Jonny said, turning his key in the front door lock. "Before they give you the keys to the kingdom, they make you sweep the floors. That's what my mom always says anyway. Come on, let's go to the practice room," Jonny said.

He led us to the back of the house, which had a tiny sun porch. There was a Japanese Fender Strat, a keyboard, and a lame Crate amp, which Jonny and I both plugged into. Ugh, Crate amps: the bottom of the barrel.

"Sorry," Jonny said. "This isn't exactly the awesome setup we have at your parents' place."

"That's okay," I said, hoping that he couldn't read my mind about the Crate amp.

"Your dad has that Vox. And the Dual Showman, and the seventies Marshall combo. Those amps are so sweet!"

"Totally," I said. "You can play through them anytime. He doesn't mind."

"Cool, thanks. The Showman has a tremolo channel, right?" Jonny was getting all excited. There was spit at the corners of his lips, he was talking so fast. Weird. I had thought I was going to be jealous of Jonny's big house, but instead he was literally drooling over my dad's gear.

"Yep."

"But not a presence button?"

"No, I think those were only on silver-faces. His is a black-face."

"Right, right."

"I have absolutely no idea what you're talking about," Crackers said.

☆

We did a run-through of "Belle's Metal Riff," and although it desperately needed drums, at least it sounded tight. Then Jonny showed us a chord progression he had written. I didn't point out that for someone supposedly not interested in being *in* this band, Jonny now appeared to be positioning himself as a contributing songwriter. Why mention it? He was putting enough of himself into this project that by the time he got the willies and tried to pull out, he'd be in too deep. I'd have him in my clutches soon, so I opted for a mellower approach.

"Cool song," I said. "Maybe we could do this one in Don Daddio's battle."

Jonny didn't even look up, just kept watching his fingers on the fret board. But I could tell he'd heard every word.

Christine and I joined in on the chords, experimenting with different ideas until something clicked. Jonny even took a pretty good solo, but his slip-sliding glasses kept getting in the way. He'd play a few notes, then have to push the glasses back up his nose. He'd play another little phrase, then push them up again. I couldn't help but point it out.

"It kind of helps me solo better," Jonny said. "Like, I have all these different ideas, but I don't want to cram them in all at once. My glasses help me stretch them out a little bit instead." So maybe in some ways it helps to have nerdish tendencies when you're learning how to rock.

"Oops," he said after hitting a bad note. "Bungle." I had never heard the expression before.

"What does that mean?" I asked.

"It means I screwed up," Jonny said.

"Sounded about right to me."

Next, Crackers showed us a Stevie Wonder song, "A Place in the Sun," which she played note for note perfectly. Every last Rhodes piano trill was in the right place, and the feeling was so soulful and right on that I could almost picture Little Stevie doing his crazy-happy head-bobbing moves right there in Jonny's studio. I laid down a tight bass line that worked fine, and Jonny added some *wah-wah* guitar. We played that thing for at least a half hour before calling it quits.

"Let's make a snack," Jonny said. It was almost five. "Lunch is a distant memory."

"Cool. I'm starving," I said.

Crackers kept tinkering at the keyboard. "You want us to make you something and bring it back?" Jonny asked.

"Sure. Thanks."

We walked to the kitchen and Jonny opened the fridge.

"Organic," Jonny said, pulling out a half-eaten roast chicken, Muenster cheese, and mayo. He grabbed a loaf of bread from the countertop and started making sandwiches.

"When do your parents get home?" I asked.

"Um, a quarter to never. The midterm's almost here. My mom'll get home by seven probably, and my dad will stroll in at midnight, make himself a chicken sandwich like this, then pass out in bed. Family togetherness. It's awesome."

"Your parents sound exactly like mine," I said. "Hey, watch it with that junk"—I pointed to the mayo in Jonny's hand before he could contaminate my sandwich with it—"I can't stand mayo."

"My parents are total nerds who talk for hours and hours about stuff nobody cares about," Jonny said. "Yours play rock music and get paid to do it. They must be the coolest parents on the face of the earth."

"Trust me, they may *look* cool, but as parents they're probably just as lame as yours. Probably lamer."

I turned toward the sun porch and yelled, "Christine, you into mayo or mustard?" but didn't get an answer.

"Let's bring everything down to the practice room," Jonny said. "We can bring her both, on the side."

When we got back, Crackers was still playing the Stevie Wonder song, but the surprising thing was, she was also singing. She had her back turned to us, so she didn't know we were behind her, and she was really putting her heart into it. At first, she sang quietly, but right away I could tell she was something special. By the second verse, Crackers was in her own spacey world, and she really turned up the volume. She sang that song six ways from Sunday.

Christine, *the* awkward beanpole Christine, the classical music geek from another planet, had a great—no, a *phenomenal*—voice. It was strong, enormous, way bigger than anything you could expect to come out of the mouth of a skinny dork like her. But it also sounded almost like crying—sad, lonely, wise. For such a beautiful thing, it was almost scary.

"Whoa," said Jonny, in a low-key but also seriously impressed way. Crackers turned around and faced him. "Guess we've found the lead singer."

Huh? I thought. Christine was obviously *not* going to become the lead singer. Not on my watch. I was as impressed as Jonny was, but I wasn't about to relinquish my lead singer status to an upstart with crumbs on her shirt.

"You're really good," I said, with some effort.

"Thanks," Christine said.

"Where'd you learn to do that?" Jonny said.

"In church, I guess. But the choir's so big, I can barely hear myself." Her eyes widened. "Oooh, is that roast chicken?"

"This girl has some serious lungs," Jonny said.

"Slow down, Jonny," I said. "You're not even in this band, remember?" I strapped on Satomi, walked over to the Showman, and turned it up a notch. What I lacked in talent, I could make up for in sheer volume.

OPEN MIC

The following Wednesday, Ronaldo pinged me.

> EggMtnRckr: So, JONNY thought her voice was sweet . . .
> what'd YOU think?!?
> **Bassinyrface: I dont know, pretty good, I guess.**
> EggMtnRckr: Well, that rules, then. She can be the J
> Lennon to your P McCartney.
> **Bassinyrface: yeah, maybe.**
> EggMtnRckr: Listen, the more good people you have,
> the better yr band's gonna be.
> **Bassinyrface: I guess.**
> EggMtnRckr: And Jonny's playing well?
> **Bassinyrface: Yeah, but he's not even really IN
> the band. Blech.**

EggMtnRckr: I think youre just mad because he went off about how great Crackers voice is.

Bassinyrface: meh.

EggMtnRckr: seriously you should be PSYCHED that you found an amazing singer.

Bassinyrface: that's easy for you to say, you get to be the singer.

EggMtnRckr: she can sing some sings, YOU can sing some songs. Dont forget, youre still the leader as long as youre writing songs.

I didn't tell EggMtnRckr that I still wasn't exactly writing songs. Fragments? Sure. Snippets? Maybe. But not full-blown songs. Not yet.

☆

As I walked into the kitchen to make a snack, I heard my mom's voice. She was talking on the phone in a tense, quiet voice in front of the sink, so I stayed in my room and tried to listen in.

"No, I guess I didn't realize how bad it was for them . . . No, I understand," she said in a shaky voice. "But do you really think we should even *consider* that?"

She didn't speak for a few seconds. I couldn't figure out who she was talking to. Someone from my school, or X's? Some social worker, butting in and making problems?

"It's true, X is having some real issues lately. He seems to be regressing. He's acting very childish and it's hard to know how to give him what he needs." She paused to listen. "And Belle is dealing with a lot of anger right now. She's mad at us for bringing her up here, for taking her away from her friends and her band, and she's not adjusting to her new school very well."

If you don't think I have self-control, guess again, because it took every ounce of restraint for me not to run into the kitchen and flip out at this totally incorrect statement.

"Yes, Marielis, I know you are putting their best interests first. I know how much you love them."

Marielis—it was Abuela! What was she talking about? I mean, I was glad that she seemed to be telling my mom off, but what were they "considering"? And why weren't X and I a part of the discussion?

"I will discuss it with them, Marielis, and we'll come up with a game plan, okay? Thank you so much for your concern . . . Okay, then . . . Bye-bye."

☆

I walked over to Jonny's locker on Friday, hoping to catch him between classes, and found a note taped there. It was folded in half and said "BEWARE" in big Gothic letters. There was a very well-drawn skull and crossbones on it. I tried to put myself in Jonny's shoes. If he just happened to find a potential death threat taped to my locker five minutes before I did, would I mind if he ripped it off and looked at it? After all, he could warn me before I stepped on a booby trap. He could shove me to the ground if .22 caliber bullets were about to whiz by my head. It was my duty to read this note.

"I hear you've picked up your guitar again," it read in blunt Magic Marker black. "Do us both a favor and put it back down. Forever."

It wasn't signed. Had to be Jackson, though, right? But why? Why would he care if Jonny was playing with us?

"What's up, Belle?" It was Jonny. I turned around, not too fast, holding the note at my side like it was nothing.

"Not much. Just wanted to say what's up." There was no way he saw me take it down, I figured, so unless I panicked I wouldn't get caught in this obvious error in judgment. I'd just circle back after the bell rang and tape it back up, and he'd see it after next period. No big deal.

"You see Of Montreal on *Late Night* last night?" Jonny asked.

"Nope. I was in bed by eleven," I said.

"They were sweet."

"I believe it."

"Practice at yours this weekend?"

"Yep."

"Let's record that Crackers song! The Stevie Wonder one."

"Meh. I don't know if my parents' mics are still up. We'll see."

After we parted ways, I made sure he was good and gone and taped the note back up. If he needed help, if he needed all the protection my midget-sized frame could offer, he would ask.

☆

The Soundtrack of My Life, by Annabelle Cabrera
Opening Credits: "The Perfect Me," Deerhoof
Receiving a Gift: "Strawberry Fields Forever," The Beatles
Treasured Memory: "Kooks," David Bowie
Disagreement: "Misery Is a Butterfly," Blonde Redhead

Making Up: "Seven Seas," Echo and the Bunnymen
Moment of Regret: "Waitin' for a Superman," The Flaming Lips
The Happy Dance: "Wrong Time Capsule," Deerhoof
Loneliness: "Nowhere Man," The Beatles
The Final Battle: "Declare Independence," Björk
Closing Credits: "Crimson and Clover," Joan Jett

I came to class with my final list—told you I was retro. I had slaved on it for about two hours, going through my iPod over and over in search of the ten songs that express everything that is Annabelle Cabrera. But Mr. V didn't even want to see it.

"Okay, students, now for part two," he said. "I want you to write journal entries." McNamara groaned super loudly and Mr. V raised an eyebrow in his direction. "This will be a sort of song journal, an explanation of at least one paragraph—that's three sentences or more, Mr. McNamara—in which you justify your choice of each particular song. Think of it as something you might one day give to your own child as a way of explaining who you were in sixth grade. Unless your soundtrack includes classics like Bon Jovi, these young people of the future will have little idea of the musicians you admired so long ago. So don't bother explaining the music. Just get to the feelings they evoke. Use the songs to paint a *portrait of yourself* in these, the ancient days in which you live."

I glanced at Crackers's soundtrack as we filed out of class. She had "A Place in the Sun" for her final battle and "Hey Jude" for her moment of regret. I didn't recognize any of the other songs. Three of them had Jesus in the title, so they must have been from church.

☆

Our confusingly nonofficial band had practice at my place on Sunday afternoon.

"Let's run through 'A Place in the Sun,'" Jonny said as he plugged in, having no idea that this was Christine's battle song.

I didn't respond. It was annoying that he was so into Christine's voice. She had a great one, but big deal. One nice voice and three cover songs do not make a band great. We had written only one real song so far, and it barely even had a chorus. What was the point of screwing around recording Crackers when we didn't even have original material yet?

"Earth to Annabelle Cabrera. Let's run through it, okay?" Jonny repeated. Crackers just stood there, playing chords with her headphones on, completely oblivious to the tension in the room.

"Let's play 'Metal Riff' first. I want to try some new lyrics," I said.

"Okay."

We played "Metal Riff." And that's exactly what it sounded like. A riff. Not a song, just a riff.

"This sucks," I said.

"What? I like it," said Jonny.

Crackers didn't say anything.

"I need to keep working on the lyrics."

"Okay. Whatever. Let's play the Christine song. I want to

try an acoustic guitar part on it." *The Christine song?* Ugh. Jonny picked up my dad's acoustic and tuned it.

Crackers played the opening chords to "A Place in the Sun," and Jonny joined in on guitar. I came in on bass, and we sounded good. A little boring, a little old-fashioned, but tight. Crackers started to sing.

I heard keys in the front door. Out of the corner of my eye, I saw my dad enter the apartment and take an immediate right up the loft stairs. But after a few steps, he came back down again. He leaned around my amp and began to spy on our practice. Christine started the second verse. Her eyes closed as she wrapped her booming, velvety voice around the song.

I admit it. She sounded amazing. My dad came out from behind the amp. Shaky Jake and my mom were at his side. Great. Crackers's voice was clear as a bell as she reached the climax of the song. She had a way of sliding up into the notes that could make goose bumps appear all over your body. She sang the words like she really meant them. At one point, Jake gave out a hearty "Yeah!" But when the song was over, the room went quiet. I expected cheers, applause . . . *something*.

Nobody said a word. Then, finally, Mom spoke.

"Honey, you have the most amazing voice!" she said, looking right at Christine. *Honey?*

"Nice job, seriously!" said Shaky Jake.

"I can't believe a twelve-year-old can sing with that much soul," added my dad.

"Actually, I'm eleven," Christine said.

"You are?" said Jonny.

"I skipped a grade."

"Well, you've got quite a voice on you," said my dad. "What was your name again?"

"Crackers 'n' Cheese," I said.

"Christine," Jonny said, shooting me a look.

"Well, Christine, you have got something pretty special there," my dad said. "Jake, maybe she could double your vocals on 'Trouble in Mind.' What do you think?"

"Babe, the record's already mixed and mastered," said my mom. "We can't just go back and add more parts to it."

"What did everybody think about the *band*?" I said. I could feel my face going pink, then red. I had throat-sewn-shut syndrome again and could barely get the words out. "How did the *band* sound?"

"Well . . . you sounded great," said my mom.

"Absolutely," said my dad. "You played wonderfully."

"You had a little bit of a Jackson Five thing going on, which, believe me, is a huge compliment," said Jake.

That was pretty weak, I thought. Other than Michael, what did the other Jacksons ever do?

"You mean, we sound like a kid band?" I said.

"Look, Annabelle, you guys are a band trying to find its own sound, and you *sound* like a band still trying to find its own sound," said my dad. "But you've got yourself a pretty amazing lead singer here. Congratulations, kiddo, you've got an eye for talent."

Something snapped inside me. I had to get out of that room immediately. I didn't exactly throw Satomi to the floor, but I wasn't being too careful, either, and I dropped her. A sharp squawk of feedback pierced through the amp.

"Belle, where are you going?" asked Jonny.

"Shut up, Jonny."

I had to get out of there, and I had to edge my way between my dad and Jake to do it. They looked really shocked and embarrassed, which made me even more upset, and as I pushed past Jake, I did something that I would immediately regret, especially because it was the second time I'd done it in ten days. I slapped him on the shoulder. I must have done it pretty hard, because he winced in pain.

"What did I do?" he moaned, shaking out his arm.

"Annabelle, come back here and apologize to Jake. Right now," said my mom.

This was a moment when an actual room would have been extremely useful, because I really needed a door to slam. Instead, I slammed the bathroom door on my *way* to my "personal area," then put my iPod on and crashed on my bed. Crackers was not going to be the star of *my* group, and I was not going to be just some backup musician in a Stevie Wonder cover band!

I don't really know how long Jonny and Crackers stayed, but I eventually fell asleep. When I woke up, the clock read 1:15 a.m. My parents were still up, talking quietly but tensely in the kitchen, and X was snoring away on the other side of the screen. Even in the middle of the night, I couldn't get any peace or privacy.

Annabelle's most important rock rule of all:
Rock stars always *get their own room.*

☆

"Annabelle, wake up, sweetie. Wake up."

I was dreaming that I was on an amusement park ride

called the Kamikaze. I had gone on it once in New Jersey visiting my uncle, and I had never forgotten it. It's like a subway car connected to a giant rotating arm. You get crammed in there with about fifteen other people you don't know, the arm starts to move, and you suddenly realize you've made a huge mistake. But there's no escape. You're upside down and careening around and around, and two minutes feel like four hours. You're trapped and you think it's never going to end. In my dream, my seat belt started to vibrate, and my chair started shaking around, but I think it was just my mom lightly squeezing my shoulder as she tried to get me out of bed.

"Wake up, sleepyhead," she said. "You feeling any better?"

"I'm okay, I guess. What time is it?"

"It's six forty-five. In the morning. You slept over twelve hours."

"What happened to Jonny and Christine?"

"Well, I offered to make them something to eat, but they said they had to get home and left about ten minutes after your . . . exit. What was that all about, Belle?"

"I don't know. I mean, it's *my* band. I put it together. And we're practicing in *my* house, in front of *my* parents. She's not even that great of a singer." Ha, what a lie.

"Belle, I thought you played great. You're a great bassist, and you're just getting started."

See, my mom could be cool sometimes. Once in a while, she actually said the right thing at the right time. But I still wasn't satisfied.

"That wasn't even the kind of song I want to play, though. That's a *gospel* song. I want to rock."

"Belle, very few musicians actually wind up in the band they thought they wanted to be in. Take Shaky Jake. You know what his favorite band is?"

That was easy. "ZZ Top."

"Exactly. Blues guitar and foot-long beards. What does ZZ Top have in common with Benny and Joon?"

"Absolutely nothing."

"Right. Your dad found Jake in a deadbeat blues bar called Kenny's Castaways. Jake had never even heard the kind of music we asked him to play. And to this day, I don't even know if he's a Benny and Joon fan. But when we met him, we clicked. It was like he was part of the family from the second he stepped through the door." She paused, grazing her fingers lightly through my hair, tucking it behind my ear. "So, what do you think of Jonny and Christine? They seem so nice. Do you like them?"

"Yeah. I do."

"Then maybe you need to let go a little bit and let your band become the band that represents all three of you guys, instead of just you."

"So you think if I form a band that represents all three of us, Dad will start to acknowledge my existence? Or will he just invite Crackers to be the new singer of Benny and Joon?"

"Annabelle, stop. Your father didn't mean anything by that. He just gets excited when he spots new talent."

"I'm a new talent, and I'm sitting right under his nose."

Then, out of nowhere, my mom knelt down on the floor and, leaning against the side of my bed, burst into tears.

"Mom, what's wrong?" I said. "What did I say?"

"You didn't say anything, Belle." She wiped the tears away

and tried to get it together. "It's just that I need to ask you something. Something very serious."

This is what she and Abuela were talking about on the phone. It had to be.

"What, Mom?" I asked.

She cried for a few seconds more, then shook her head to get rid of the tears for good. "Would you rather live here, with your father and me, or would you rather move back to Brooklyn?"

"And live with Abuela?" I asked. "Where would X go? Would he go with me, or stay with you?"

"I don't know, honey. We haven't thought it through yet. I haven't even spoken to your dad about any of this. I wanted to talk to you first."

"I don't know, Mom. It's been really, really hard here. I miss Abuela, and Ronaldo, and actually being in a band instead of banging my head against the wall trying to start a new one."

"I know, Belle, I know. I'm sorry we had to take you away from your friends and your music."

"And my grandmother."

"And your grandmother."

"It would be weird to live without you and Dad."

She was doing everything she could not to cry. It wasn't really working.

"Yes," she said. "It would be really difficult for us, too. But we want you to be happy."

Then she really lost it, burying her head in my pillow and lying down next to me in my bed. I petted her head a little and told her it would be okay, which was totally weird. Shouldn't she have been the one comforting and petting me?

I told her I needed to think about it. Move back to Brooklyn? The idea filled me with a joy I hadn't felt since we'd moved here. But would it be the same to go back? Would Ronaldo even want me in Egg Mountain if it meant kicking out Anthony? Would X come with me? Would I miss my parents? I was too confused to answer *any* of these questions.

So instead of doing what I would normally do in this situation—pace around the room like a nut while talking to myself—I decided to try to write out my frustration. I woke up my computer and quickly worked on my Mr. V assignment:

I chose "Declare Independence," the Björk song, for my final battle song because when she sings this song, she sounds like she is at war. Maybe not the kind of war where you load up guns, fly flags, and climb mountaintops. But maybe the kind of war where sometimes it feels like everybody is standing between you and your dream, and you have to get a little bit mad in order to become who you want to be.

All my life people have used annoying words to describe me, like "sassy" or "spunky." I hate the word "spunky." It sounds like a word for feeling like you want to throw up. People describe Björk as spunky, too. (Or they just talk about how she wears weird clothes.) Sassy and spunky mean full of energy and attitude. But I don't really feel like I have attitude. I feel like I will never get what I want in life. I will never be able to lead my own band. I will never be able to do what Ronaldo did, not on my own. I will never be noticed again, by my parents or anyone else. I will be invisible.

I don't know what possessed me to write this, especially right after my mom broke down and told me I might be moving back to Brooklyn. It wasn't a song exactly, this rant about my life. But maybe I'd be able to look at it in a few hours, or a few days, and turn it into a song. Maybe I could turn this upside-down fall into something positive. I had to do *something*, because the way things were now was making me crazy.

☆

Later that night, I pinged R:

EggMtnRckr: My advice on Crackers . . . totally forget what your dad thinks. Who cares, you know?

Bassinyrface: I cant believe i'm hearing this from the guy who basically worships my dad. as a musician, anyway.

EggMtnRckr: well, that doesnt mean he knows everything.

Bassinyrface: so youre saying you think I'm a better singer than Crackers?

EggMtnRckr: Wha?!? How would I know that? I've never even heard her.

Bassinyrface: Grrr.

EggMtnRckr: Here's what I'm trying to say . . . I've never heard C sing before, but I've heard YOU sing before, and I know YOU are a good singer.

Bassinyrface: Ok. Thanks.

EggMtnRckr: First thing is, you should try not to compare yrself to other people all the time. Just worry about getting better at what you do: PLAY BASS, SING, and most importantly WRITE SWEEEET SONGS.

Bassinyrface: but in Egg Mountain I was a major part of the band. I had, like, followers!

EggMtnRckr: you liked being the center of attention, huh?

Bassinyrface: Well, not THE center of attention, but A center of attention. Yeah, why not?!?

EggMtnRckr: Did you ever think about how I felt when I'd been working on Egg Mountain for over a year, dreaming about it for years before that, and then this upstart girl comes along, sings a song or two, and starts getting HER OWN FANS?!?!?

Bassinyrface: umm, no. I guess I hadn't.

EggMtnRckr: Well, at first it was kind of hard, to be honest. But then I realized that having you around only made the band better, so I kinda coached myself into not worrying about it.

Bassinyrface: That's totally cool! I had no idea. Thanks, R.

EggMtnRckr: Rule number six: DONT COMPETE WITH YR OWN BANDMATES! ☺

Bassinyrface: I know, I know.

EggMtnRckr: Just joking you, Belle, dont sweat it. Just be glad that not only do you have YOUR awesome talent, you have Crackers too!

Bassinyrface: Absolutely. Youre right, R. As usual.

EggMtnRckr: So youre gonna help me out next time I have a band crisis of my own, right?
Bassinyrface: Yes, yes, yes! Absolutely. I swear. Double swear. TRIPLE SWEAR!!!

I was going to mention the Brooklyn possibility to Ronaldo, but I was too nervous to do it. I mean, what if he loved Anthony's playing so much that he'd tell me I was out of Egg Mountain, now and forever? I was too freaked out to deal with that, so I tried to act as if the choice of Brooklyn didn't even exist. I went about my life as if the conversation with my mom hadn't happened, figuring that soon enough the right decision would come to me.

☆

My mom asked me to take the bus with X again and drop him off on the way to school. Awesome! X was in the exact opposite mood as me, and obviously clueless about what had gone on between my mom and me the night before. I was feeling quiet and mellow and wanted to take things nice and slow. He, on the other hand, was swinging in the center of the aisle, grabbing the tops of two seats in opposite rows and barely keeping his balance while swinging. If it hadn't been so irritating, I would have been pretty impressed by his athletic feat. X looked like he was about to begin one of those old-school break-dancing routines that you sometimes see teenage kids do on the subways in New York. I wondered if he was going to start spinning in circles on the floor as a way to earn extra change.

Then my phone vibrated three times: a message. I looked at the missed call and saw that Abuela had called only thirty seconds before. And when I called back, of course, she didn't pick up. Stupid cell phone! Was it just me or was the reception in Providence twice as bad as in Brooklyn? Finally, I shrugged and listened to the message.

"Hello, my Annabella," she said. "Oh, honey, I'm miss you so much right now and I'm wondering, do you talk to your mommy this morning about anything special? Call me when you feel you want talk, okay, honey?"

I couldn't call her back; I didn't know what to say yet. I didn't know what to say because I didn't know what to do. Providence, or Brooklyn? As The Clash once sang, "Should I stay or should I go?"

Rock stars always know exactly what they want.

☆

"Guys, I'm sorry I freaked out," I said to Jonny and Christine in front of Christine's locker. "I shouldn't have stormed out like that."

"You did freak out," said Jonny. "And you told me to shut up. Not cool."

"I'm really sorry. It had nothing to do with you. That was between me and my parents."

"Remember when I said how bands bring out the worst in people?"

"Yeah, I do. It won't happen again."

"If you don't want me to be the singer, I can just be the keyboard player," said Christine.

"No, no. I want you to sing," I said. "Really."

"How about you both sing?" said Jonny. "Duh. Harmonies. Two girl vocalists. You'll be huge."

Crackers and I looked at each other.

"Okay," I said. "We'll both sing."

"How about working on something for this?" Christine said, pointing to a poster across the hall. It was for an open-mic concert at next Friday's lunch assembly. Anyone could play. All we had to do was sign up.

"We don't even have a drummer. We're not even a band yet," I said.

"You don't even have a guitarist yet," Jonny said. "Remember, I said I'd practice, but no gigs."

"You guys are wimps," Crackers said.

"What?" I said.

"You say you want to be in a band, but you're afraid. Both of you."

"I am not afraid," I said.

"I might be a little afraid," Jonny said.

"Annabelle, what are you more interested in?" Christine asked. "Forming a band, or looking cool? Because we might not look that cool at this open mic, but if we do well, people will notice us. And what better way is there to find a drummer than to show the whole school that we're serious about playing?"

"She has a point," said Jonny.

"The drummers will come to *us*," Christine said.

"So, Jonny, you'll do it if I do it?"

I looked for a flicker of doubt on his face. He had to have seen the threatening note by now, so he knew there was some risk involved if he played in public with us.

"Okay, I'll do it. I'm a hired gun, though. Just till you find somebody permanent."

We both knew that he'd said he'd never perform with us before. And now he was a *willing participant* in a live show. So he wasn't exactly saying yes to being in our band. But he wasn't exactly saying no, either.

HEY, CRACKERS

On Friday, two periods before the lunch assembly and the open mic, Mr. V gave us back our Soundtrack of My Life song lists, complete with the descriptions of why we had picked the songs. He had already said that "this exercise is not a judgment on your musical taste," but I was still a little worried about having my excellent indie song list critiqued by a middle-aged Bon Jovi fan. Plus, good song choices were all I had! I felt like I had only actually done a good job on four of the songs and just scribbled random stuff under the other ones, so I braced myself for a horrible grade. But when I looked down, I saw a big fat A at the top of the page. Plus, there were exclamation marks next to every paragraph that I had actually completed. He must have really loved it!

The Soundtrack of My Life, by Annabelle Cabrera
Opening Credits: "The Perfect Me," Deerhoof
Everyone dreams of being perfect at something. It could be school, or sports, or Grand Theft Auto. I want to be as perfect as Satomi Matsuzaki at playing the bass, singing, jumping around, and generally being awesome. This is my favorite Deerhoof song of all time. The drums are crazy, there are weird bell sounds on top of everything, and a church organ from outer space.

Receiving a Gift: "Strawberry Fields Forever," The Beatles
This is my "receiving a gift" song because that's how I feel when I'm listening to it: like I am being given a gift by The Beatles. Directly by The Beatles, like they wrote it just for me. It's a really gentle song, but then every once in a while Ringo's drums really bang in on a fill, and it just sounds awesome. I also like how a lot of the words don't really mean anything. But if you know the song, they somehow do start to make sense. They make sense the way a beautiful dream makes sense, but then you wake up and you can't explain to anybody *what made the dream so excellent.*

Treasured Memory: "Kooks," David Bowie
This song reminds me of how life was when I was really young, maybe four or six years old or something. The song's about a couple of weirdos who are in love—and trust me, my parents are kind of weird—and who have a

kid. Maybe by accident, it's hard to tell. But they are happy about having the baby, and they sing a song to her, welcoming her to their nutty family. The parents in the song sort of apologize for being weird, and to make up for it they buy the kid a trumpet and a guide for how to not get picked on, which is totally something I could use right now.

And it's cool to be different, but I wish my parents were more like they used to be, more like the parents in this Bowie song. When we lived in Brooklyn, with my abuela, she was the boss, and my parents and brother and I were kind of all her kids. It was a lot more fun that way.

Moment of Regret: "Waitin' for a Superman," The Flaming Lips

Sometimes you just want somebody to come down and save you. Maybe you're having a bad day. Maybe you wish you were taller or played the bass better. But you can't just become an amazing musician or grow a whole foot overnight, so you dream about it instead. I think I chose this for "moment of regret" because I always used to think my dad was Superman, and then one day I woke up and realized he was just my dad. He was just a guy.

Loneliness: "Nowhere Man," The Beatles

What I love about Beatles songs is that the words can be really sad sometimes, but it doesn't matter because you feel happy when you listen to the melodies and instruments. Everybody feels lonely sometimes, but I never feel lonely when I listen to The Beatles, because it's like they're kind of holding your hand and helping you through the hard times. You might be lonely when you turn on this song, but three minutes later you realize it's all going to be okay.

Final Battle: "Declare Independence," Björk
I chose "Declare Independence," the Björk song, for my final battle song because when she sings this song, she sounds like she is at war. Maybe not the kind of war where you load up guns, fly flags, and climb mountaintops. But maybe the kind of war where sometimes it feels like everybody is standing between you and your dream, and you have to get a little bit mad in order to become who you want to be.

All my life people have used annoying words to describe me, like "sassy" or "spunky." I hate the word "spunky." It sounds like a word for feeling like you want to throw up. People describe Björk as spunky, too. (Or they just talk about how she wears weird clothes.) Sassy and spunky mean full of energy and attitude. But I don't really feel like I have attitude. I feel like I will never get what I want in life. I will never be able to lead my own band. I will never be able to do what Ronaldo did, not on my own. I will never be noticed again, by my parents or anyone else. I will be invisible.

Closing Credits: "Crimson and Clover," Joan Jett
Tommy James wrote this song around the time my parents were born, but Joan Jett did it in the eighties and totally owned it. She's somebody who would do another person's

song note for note but still somehow makes it all her own. I really don't know how everything in the lyrics adds up to "Crimson and Clover," but those words just sound so good together! Oh, Joan, how I love thee. The guitars on this record are HUGE, but her voice goes back and forth between hard and soft, tough and gentle. When she's barely whispering on top of those crunchy, distorted guitar chords, I feel like I'm lying in a field of grass gazing up at a blue sky so wide open and unending, it almost hurts.

"This is great, even though you still owe me some of the assignment," Mr. V wrote. "You are finally opening up a little bit here. We are seeing the real Annabelle now. This is what good writers do. But it's still not complete. Keep going!"

The real Annabelle? I read my final battle paragraph again and felt a rush of warmth spread across my face. "I will be invisible," I had written. It was just embarrassing.

"Okay, class," Mr. V said. "Now comes the hard part: creating a work of art. Over the weekend, I want you to look again at what you have written. Many of you have written very well so far, but in a rather unstructured way. Your thoughts and expressions are full of life on these pages, but they are still raw. The next step is to use your soundtrack as inspiration to create a work of art, a finished piece that you are proud of, a piece that says something of who . . . you . . . are."

I'm not sure if anyone knew what he was talking about. I waited until all the other kids had filed out to approach Mr. V's desk.

"Ah, Ms. Cabrera," he said. "Nice work on that assignment. Do you know what your work of art will be?"

"Huh?" I said.

"Your work of art. A song perhaps?"

"Yep, that's what I want to do. But . . ."

"It's scary, right?"

"No, I'm not scared exactly. I've been around songwriting my whole life. My parents do it, my friends do it. And when they do it, it looks really easy. Every time I do it, though, it feels impossible."

"So you've written songs before, then?"

"Well, that's the thing. I just write a few words here, a few words there. I put them to some chords. Sometimes it sounds good, but I can never finish anything. The ideas never *go* anywhere."

"Ah, you've got a bit of a block happening, maybe. It takes a long while to truly become good at something, you know. You might not feel very young right now, but believe me, you are. And you have a lot of time to develop your talents. The only thing I can say is that, as your teacher, I see you have a lot to say. You just need to keep working at it, a little bit every day. It's a long climb, but believe me, you will get there. Slow and steady wins the race."

☆

Slow and steady wins the race. As I set up my bass and looked out at the bleachers, I tried to take courage from Mr. V's saying, but at that moment it just didn't do the trick. These assemblies were a total drag. Teachers stood in the halls like watchdogs, making sure each and every kid filed into the gym, but for what? To hear an endless list of boring announcements from the principal, or maybe a motivational speech from the art teacher about how beautiful autumn could be if you only looked up and noticed the trees' changing leaves. Mostly, they were an excuse for boys to yell out jokes and see if they could get the crowd laughing. I guess the hopeful part of me thought this open mic might change the mood of the assembly, but it hadn't at all. If anything, the jokers were *more* amped up than usual—this time they had a chance to make fun of their own classmates.

This performance was going to be a huge, humiliating mistake. The stand-up comic and the juggler who had also signed up had dropped out earlier that morning, so we were the only act stupid enough to subject ourselves to the open-mic treatment. Half the crowd looked bored out of their minds, and the rest of the kids were hurling insults our way:

"Loser!"

"Beatles Geek!"

"Dork!"

"Crackers 'n' Cheeeeeeeese!"

"Fatty McGoth!"

I don't know how they even recognized Jonny, though. He wore sunglasses and a baseball cap so low on his head that I wasn't sure he'd be able to see his guitar strings.

"Is that a disguise?" I asked him.

"Kind of." Either he knew that doing the open mic was the biggest dork maneuver in history or he was hiding from Jackson. Or whoever else might have written him the threatening note.

Mrs. Harris, the principal, played the MC role.

"Okay, kids, we have something really special for today's open mic," she said. "It's a new rock group of sixth graders."

Jonny's disguise must have been successful, because Harris didn't realize that a full-blown seventh grader was our guitarist, even though he was too embarrassed to be seen with us.

"I don't believe they have a name." She turned to us. "What do you call yourselves?"

"IDIOTS!" somebody yelled from the stands.

"Hey!" Harris yelled. I didn't know she had it in her. She was serious about this hope-and-love thing. "These kids have the floor!" Then she walked off and the floor was ours indeed.

Jonny plunked out the intro chords of "Hey Jude" so quietly that I couldn't even hear the beat, and I was two feet away from him. Then he flubbed a D chord and stopped dead in his tracks.

"Oops," he said. "Bungle."

"They should be called The Bungles!" said the jerk from the stand. Half the audience cracked up. Were we going to be the first band in history to be named by a heckler? Maybe. But I was not going to let Rule Number Five get the best of me!

"Go ahead, Jonny," I whispered. "Start it again."

He played the intro again, more confidently, and Christine and I joined in. I sang the first verse, and I sounded okay, I thought. There were a couple more heckles, but by the time I was done with my part of the song, everybody had shut up. I remembered this from the Egg Mountain days, the way a good song played by a good band can silence a restless, obnoxious crowd in seconds. Music is a powerful thing, and even our quiet little Beatles cover was working its power.

But by the time Crackers finished *her* first verse, she absolutely owned the crowd.

"Go, Crackers!" yelled out a high-sounding girl's voice. I was thinking, *Crackers has a groupie?*

I had pushed for "Hey Jude" instead of "A Place in the Sun" to avoid having Crackers look *so* much better than me, but it didn't make a difference. She was amazing, no matter what song she sang. This much was clear: Crackers was going to be the star of this band. As I scanned the bleachers, I saw that half the kids had stood up. Most of the school had probably never even consciously laid their eyes on this gawky girl, a mere eleven-year-old who blended into the sea of faces in the halls. Before today, there had been nothing unique about her except for her constant snacking. Plus, she was all spindly arms and legs, and had that distant quality, that faraway look in her eyes of someone who barely even seemed to know where she was.

But when she sang, none of that mattered. I watched her as she went into the *nah nah nah nahs* of the outro, and I could tell she wasn't even *trying* to hit it out of the park. It just came naturally to her. She followed where the music took her, and when I listened to her sing "Hey Jude," it was like I was hearing the song's true meaning for the first time, feeling all the emotion that Paul McCartney must have felt when he had written it. Crackers reached deep into the heart of the lyrics about cheering up a sad little boy, and made it sound like a love letter to the whole school. I was blown away. So was Jonny, and so was the audience. Christine, without even trying, had everybody eating out of the palm of her hand.

"Crackers! Crackers! Crackers!" the audience chanted. Suddenly the lamest nickname in the history of man had been transformed into total coolness.

When we finished, the placed erupted. We bowed *three times*, and Mrs. Harris wiped a tear from her eye. "That was amazing!" she said.

As I put away my bass, the crowd was still going bonkers, and I remembered that we needed a drummer.

I walked up to the mic and said, "Hey, everybody, we need a drummer. If anybody's interested, find us in the halls!" But nobody could hear me above the chants. I looked at Jonny, and he shrugged as if to say, *Good luck, there's no way you're getting heard in this crazy scene.* So I gave up and followed Crackers and Jonny back to our seats in the stands. As we made our way through the crowd of fifth graders sitting on the floor in front of the first row of bleachers, I could see that kids were looking at all of us differently—not just at Christine, but at Jonny and me, too. They stared at us, respect in their eyes, and in Crackers's case, actual awe. I had figured we'd be either ignored or ridiculed, but never worshiped in this Egg Mountainy way. We had barely rehearsed the song and had been making mistakes up until the last minute of rehearsals. Before today, we hadn't even been worthy of teasing. Now Crackers was a full-on Federal Hill rock star, and Jonny and I stood in her glow. It wasn't quite how I'd imagined this particular scene, to say the least.

Following Crackers up the steps was like following Moses through the Dead Sea: the crowd of kids had instinctively opened up a lane for her to pass through. It was nuts, like a middle school version of the red-carpet treatment.

The three of us sat down in a row in the back, all eyes on us. Christine looked around, unsmiling and nervous.

"It's just a Beatles song," she said.

But Jonny basked in the new celebrity, beaming.

"This is awesome," he whispered. "Count me in."

"What?" I said.

"The band. I'm in. A hundred percent."

I don't know how to describe what I felt at that moment. It felt great to get noticed, and it was even better to have Jonny as a full-time member of the band. But my worst nightmare had become true: I was just the bassist. I was just a member of Crackers's backup band.

Rock stars don't play second fiddle. To anybody.

(No matter what the Rules to Rock By say!)

DARIUS THE HILARIOUS AND THE REFUGEES OF RAISING CAIN

The Monday after the open mic, I could still see people looking at me differently, like I was actually cool or something. People watched me as I went down the hall in a way they never did at PS 443, where the hip-hop kids had never heard of Egg Mountain, despite our being well-known around the city. One Federal Hill kid stopped me and said, "Nice bass playing, Annabelle." That felt good. But was I really just the bass player? Didn't anyone realize that I had *formed* this band?

The feeling boiled over in Mr. V's room, where Christine got an ovation from the entire class. "Excellent singing, Christine, really," said Mr. V, who started off the round of applause himself. I didn't pay much attention to what happened in class after that. I just sat there, doing nothing. This was lame, I admit. *She's not THAT GREAT!!!* I wanted to yell, but instead I sank into the background.

"Ms. Cabrera," said Mr. V as I was walking out. "Come here."

I stood in front of his desk, impatient, knowing he was probably going to hand out some of his E.T. wisdom. But he surprised me.

"Nice performance, young lady. But next time, I hope you'll be performing one of your *own* songs. I've heard 'Hey Jude' enough to last me *two* lifetimes."

I wondered if he would have complained if we had picked "It's My Life" or some other ridiculous Bon Jovi cover.

☆

Ronaldo pinged me that night:

EggMtnRckr: So Mr. V and I have the same master plan for you, eh?

Bassinyrface: Ha, I guess. I'm totally trying to write songs. You realize, ya? It's not so easy!

EggMtnRckr: Oh, I totally forgot. Here's some good advice my dad told me once: try writing a BAD song.

Bassinyrface: huh?

EggMtnRckr: Well, if I know you, Belle, and I obvz do . . . you probably sit down, write a little, then are mad when it doesnt sound as good as Happiness Is a Warm Gun, God Only Knows, or Hey Jude. Am I right?!?!

Bassinyrface: I'm mad when it doesn't sound as good as Deerhoof!

EggMtnRckr: exactly! U are a total perfectionist.

Bassinyrface: Yeah, I guess. I just want to write a great song, but none of them are even good.

EggMtnRckr: Here's the thing. I followed my dad's advice and it totally worked.

Bassinyrface: What do U mean, did U write a good song, or what?

EggMtnRckr: I wrote like three horrible songs, but something happened while I was doing that. Like, since I was actually trying to write a BAD song, I stopped thinking about it. I just let it come out of me.

Bassinyrface: yeah . . . and then?

EggMtnRckr: and then after writing three lame songs, I wrote a couple good ones. And the more I did it, the better the songs got. Make sense?

Bassinyrface: Yeah, I guess.

EggMtnRckr: Just try it.

Bassinyrface: K.

EggMtnRckr: So the open mic was amazing?

Bassinyrface: Yeah, except that Crackers is a total rock star now and Jonny and me are like roadies.

EggMtnRckr: she killed it, huh?

Bassinyrface: She was pretty amazing. There were people, like, crying in the audience. It was nuts.

EggMtnRckr: That's great. How'd you and J play?

Bassinyrface: Fine. It's an easy song.

EggMtnRckr: so what's the problem?

Bassinyrface: I guess I want them to clap for me . . . not for her!!! Is that so bad?!? I mean, I STARTED THIS BAND.

EggMtnRckr: Belle, you gotta get over that. It's AWESOME that people like Crackers. Now you have TWO good singers in your band, and that'll only bring more and more people to you.

Bassinyrface: yeah, I guess.

EggMtnRckr: Cheer up, Grumps!

Bassinyrface: Okay, okay, youre right! CRACKERS RAWWWKS!

EggMtnRckr: THE BUNGLES ROCK!!! Like the name, btw.

Bassinyrface: Thanks! Oh, and P.S. EGG MOUNTAIN ALSO RAWWWKS!

EggMtnRckr: Finally! Thanks for backin me up, girl!

Bassinyrface: NP. Ronaldo, how's it going with Anthony? Is he good?

EggMtnRckr: Well, he needed a little coaching at first. It took him way long to learn the songs. Not like you. You'd basically memorized our whole set list before you even played with us.

Bassinyrface: True, true. But he's settled in now?

EggMtnRckr: Yeah, he has awesome feel for the songs. I mean, he's no Annabelle Cabrera, but we're definitely happy with him now. He's doing great.

Bassinyrface: got it.

EggMtnRckr: why do you ask?

Bassinyrface: No reason, just want to make sure I left you in good hands. Catch you later, R!

EggMtnRckr: Later, Belle. Have a good one . . .

☆

The next Saturday began with a familiar request from my mom: to take care of X during a Benny and Joon gig.

"But, Mom, I've got drummer tryouts today," I said. "I've had to babysit X five weekends in a row. It's not fair."

"I know it's not. But we don't have the money for a babysitter, sweetie. You know how it is. And we have to take every gig we can get."

"Can't you bring X with you?"

"To a twenty-one-and-over club? I don't think so."

"But it's a day gig."

"There'll still be drinking in there. It's against the law for us to bring him."

"But I can't take him to Don's, either!" Don had been nice enough to let us use the percussion room for our tryouts. "He practically tore down the store last time."

"Annabelle, I'm sorry, but I can't continue this conversation. We're going to be late."

There's nothing worse than being up against someone you know is wrong but not being able to do anything about it. I knew half the stuff my parents did was bad, but what was I going to do about it? Call child services? Get X and me sent to a foster home? No way. It's not like they were beating us up or anything. They were just ignoring us. We had to deal. Plus, my mom had now given me the option of moving back to Brooklyn, so it was almost like she could get away with anything. She had offered me the perfect escape route, and if I wasn't taking it, it was my own fault.

But today, even though I hadn't yet decided if I was staying in Providence, I just wasn't in the mood to babysit. I looked over at X, who was sitting on his skateboard and unsuccessfully trying to get a spoon to hang from his nose.

He caught my eye. "Hang out with me, Belle," he said. "I'm bored."

I looked into his eyes. He looked so lonely.

And I ditched him anyway.

It was a really stupid idea, especially since we were having tryouts at Don's, where despite X's earlier outburst, I knew he would have had a pudgy, long-haired babysitter all too happy to look after him, not to mention a host of percussion instruments that would occupy him for hours. But I was tired of hanging out with him, or tired of being the only person in the family who was willing to. I hadn't been alone, truly alone, for weeks. Between school and home, where X had become nearly a daily responsibility, my only real alone time was spent for seven or eight hours in the middle of the night, with my little brother snoring just a few feet away. I was his sister, not his mom, and it wasn't my fault that his actual parents were paying even less attention to him than they were to me.

As soon as my parents left, I bailed. X would have to figure out how to spend the day alone for once.

"Don't burn the house down," was all I told him.

☆

I practically ran all the way to Don's. I was filled with hope that today might be the day the band would find its missing link.

When I turned the corner onto Thayer Street, I did a double take. It wasn't even ten a.m. yet, and there was a whole mess of kids hanging out in front of Don's, waiting to get in. They couldn't all be there auditioning for *my band*, could they? They couldn't *all* be drummers. I saw a scrawny white kid I recognized from Mr. V's class. He had long, greasy brown hair, a navy cable-knit cap pulled down tight over his forehead, and torn jeans, like a heavy metal reject from an old *Simpsons* episode. He twirled drumsticks in the air, with more than a bit of skill, and I wondered where this little guy had been for the last two months. Where had *any* of these people come from? A tiny blond girl in pink jeans and a Donnas T-shirt leaned against a wall and pounded out sidewalk paradiddles to the music playing through her ear-buds. A seriously old-looking indie rocker guy—he had to be seventeen—with a green trench coat, wild frizzy hair, and about five days of peach-fuzz growth slumped on the ground next to her. When he saw me, he perked up.

"I think that's Annabelle," he said to the stick twirler.

"Huh?"

"The Bungles' bass player."

"Hey," I said awkwardly, with a half wave. So our name really *had* stuck. But I was just the *bass player.*

Inside, there were even more of them, at least a dozen total. I knew our band's performance had made a mark at Federal Hill—it was the talk of the school for the entire week—but this was a much bigger deal than I'd ever imagined. Some of these kids weren't even from our school, but they still wanted to try out for The Bungles, *the* hot new band on the scene.

I was mad when I'd found out Christine had posted the flyers last Friday without consulting Jonny and me—Crackers had been taking more of a leadership role since the big performance—but I had to admit it had worked. The open mic had been the ultimate exposure for us, like the middle school version of a Super Bowl commercial. And Crackers had taken full advantage: the flyers were everywhere, not just around school, but all over the neighborhood, outside Italian restaurants and bakeries, cafés, and even clubs. The Bungles were the trend of the moment, like a new phone or video game that every kid in Federal Hill suddenly wanted to have, and now anybody who could put their hands on a pair of sticks wanted in on the action.

That's when my phone started vibrating in my pocket. It was our landline.

"What is it, X?" I asked.

"I'm bored!" he said. "Can I come and hang out with you?"

"No, X, I need to be alone with my band today. Watch TV, or play a game on the computer. I'll be back in two hours."

"That's what I've *been* doing. My eyes are gonna melt off my face."

"So let 'em melt," I said. "I'll be home before you know it. Byeeee." *Click.*

I walked toward the drum room, trying to relax. One deep breath, then another. With all these kids here to try out, we'd surely be able to find somebody who could do the job, be our drummer, and help us get ready for the battle of the bands, which Crackers and Jonny now talked about constantly. So why did I feel so nervous? I was on the verge of really pulling this off, bringing together a real band. But now that I was in the Church of Rock, in the center of a storm of attention surrounding *my* band, I suddenly wasn't sure I could do it. It wasn't happening any faster than things had happened for Egg Mountain, but Egg Mountain had real songs, with great hooks and interesting lyrics. We had "Belle's Metal Riff." And Egg Mountain had Ronaldo, a cool, in-control leader. The Bungles didn't have a leader. We had a guitarist who was out one week, in the next; a keyboardist who had started acting like a royal diva after one good performance; and me. The bass player.

Crackers and Jonny must have arrived early because they were already set up, and Crackers was showing Jonny a boingy little synth vamp she must have made up recently. She bobbed her head in rhythm, and Jonny played a melody on top. They didn't even see me until I waved my hands in front of them with a big callout of "Guuuuyyyys, hellllloooo!" Jonny gave me a nod, and Christine waved. I picked up my bass and joined in, jamming for a couple minutes.

Crackers had already made up a schedule for the tryouts that included all the kids, even the ones lounging around on the street. The greasy Simpsons kid, the twirler, came in first, spinning his sticks around in his hand the way he'd been doing outside. He was pretty tricky with them, sending the right one about three feet above his head like a baton, then gracefully catching it just in time to give the snare drum a mighty pop. Then he'd twirl both sticks until they were bouncing blurs darting around in the air. It was beautiful. But could he play? So far, he looked more like a magician or a juggler than a rocker, and the last thing we needed was a trickster-poser who couldn't actually hold the rhythm together.

I asked the twirler to play a beat, any beat, and he did: a straight-up hard-rock stomp in the AC/DC vein. He scanned the room, from Jonny to Crackers to me, giving us a wide smile and looking utterly relaxed. *Check me out,* he seemed to say, greasy hair pressed down under his cable-knit cap, *I'm your new drummer.* Jonny punched a stomp box with his foot and added a crunchy riff to the twirler's pounding beat. Not bad. I joined in, anchoring the bottom end, and Crackers laid a wah-wahing synth lead on top. Not bad at all. But a minute into it, Crackers stepped up to the mic and interrupted.

"Okay, cool. Can you play anything else?"

A blank stare from the twirler. "Um, like what? What do you want me to play?" He launched his sticks into the stratosphere again, but they hit the ceiling and clattered down behind him, making a racket.

"Like, can you play a shuffle beat?"

"I don't know. I guess. Sure." He reached behind me to pick up the sticks.

Christine chimed out the chords to the swinging, loose "A Place in the Sun," and Jonny and I joined her. The twirler listened for a few seconds, but not long enough, because he had no clue just how different this beat needed to be. It had to be smooth and graceful, like a gold-medal skater tracing circles in the ice. Instead, he played it like a construction dude with a jackhammer, pummeling away, sticking to the same hard-rock groove he had used before. He seemed pleased with himself, spinning his sticks in the air again and even, once, cockily winking at me. But he was the only one in the room who thought so highly of himself. I was ready to turn twirly boy loose, but Crackers beat me to it.

"Okay, thanks a lot," she said, staring dreamily just above his head. "We'll let you know what we decide."

The twirler gave her a *Really?* look, seemingly surprised that we weren't going to bum-rush him for a group hug. But

Crackers, even in the midst of her typically out-of-it dreaminess, had been very direct. The kid got the message, packing up his sticks and leaving us to get ready for the next person on the list.

"Wow, you really took charge of that one," Jonny said, laughing.

"The kid only knew one beat," Crackers said. "Imagine him on 'Hey Jude.' He'd massacre it."

"Wouldn't want to ruin a Crackers showpiece," I said under my breath.

"What?" said Crackers. I'm pretty sure she hadn't caught my obnoxious tone, but Jonny had. He rolled his eyes.

"Nothing. You're right," I said. "That kid would ruin any Beatles song he touched." I hadn't even meant to say it, it had just come out. "Oh, and sorry for calling you Crackers. Just a slip."

"I don't even mind it anymore," she said.

"You mean, not since the whole school chanted it over and over again like you're some kind of rock star?" Jonny winked at her. The traitor.

The twirler actually turned out to be one of the *more* musical kids to show up. He was a genius of modern drumming compared to some of the talentless tykes in his wake. These kids had obviously heard about us and wanted to be part of the new sensation, blah, blah, blah, but they had to be dreaming if they considered themselves musicians. The pink-jeans girl who'd been practicing her paradiddles on the pavement? Well, she might have been okay at playing her right-left-right-right patterns on a concrete drum pad, but behind the kit she just plain could not play in time. On top of that, she was so shy—she seemed positively awestruck by Crackers and couldn't even look her in the eye, looking at Jonny or me whenever Crackers asked her a question—that she could barely speak above a murmur. Even the seventeen-year-old didn't know the difference between a cowbell and a roto-tom, and he dropped his sticks every few seconds, losing his place in the song each time. There was only one more name on the list. It wasn't looking pretty.

☆

"Darius *who*?" Jonny asked.

"Darius Mould," I said. "That's what it says right here, in black and white."

We had seen it all today, ten different flavors that spelled B-A-D, in the span of a grueling two and a half hours. At this point, bummed out and exhausted as we were—I hadn't realized how tiring it would be to meet all these kids, listening to all these beginner musicians, having to send them all packing—we had nothing to lose. Why not see what this Darius kid was all about?

I had never laid eyes on such a full-on dork. He was the kind of absurd doofus you might see on a Saturday morning cartoon, usually played by a cute-kid actor for laughs. He was a big guy, with nerdy spectacles that had thick black frames and about a foot of prescription glass; an oxford shirt buttoned all the way up; worn-out corduroys with white socks pulled over each pant leg; hiking boots on his huge feet; a tight wool cap on his head; and the bushiest Albert Einstein eyebrows I had ever seen. He had an enormous schnoz, too—the nose erupted out of his face like a fifty-story skyscraper in a one-horse town. Darius the Hilarious kept touching it, too, dabbing at it every few seconds with a piece of balled-up tissue. I wondered if the thing was oozing out grease, and I shuddered as Darius put the nasty Kleenex back in his pocket and looked over at us. He flashed a nervous grin, then turned stone-cold serious just as quickly. What a freak! And yet, there was something familiar about this guy that I couldn't place.

"I just need a second," he said in his nasal, piccolo trumpet of a voice. "Just a moment, if you please. These drums badly need to be tuned. They're just the tiniest bit pitchy, they need . . ." He spoke more and more quietly, more to himself than to us before finally trailing off.

"All righty, then," I said, giving Jonny and Christine an *Is he serious?* look.

All the other kids hadn't done much setting up. They'd simply taken their seat at the drum throne, made sure the snare drum was at the right height, then started flailing away. But this guy pulled out a drum key and started tuning each and every drum. It was a lengthy process that I had seen Jake do, usually before an important recording session. And it took Jake forever. Darius whizzed right through it, tapping the outer edges of the drums, listening to each tone, then making small adjustments to the lugs before moving on.

Quite simply, the dork was a god of drumming. We threw song after song at him, and he stroked out just the right beat for each and every one. He could handle any style: metal, punk, straight-up rock, funk, blues, even country. He could play thunderously loud or ice-skater gracefully. Whatever he did, he made us sound ten times better. The three of us started to really dig in and have fun, playing a medley of just about every song we knew, then just jamming, exchanging ideas and improvising, crossing into totally new territory. I even forgot I was supposed to be annoyed at Crackers. We exchanged glances throughout this twenty-five-minute work-out, and we seemed to have the same questions on our minds: where had this guy come from, and what could we do to make sure he became *our* guy? Once we had played liter-ally every song we knew, every riff we could dream up, we put down our instruments.

"That was . . . amazing," Crackers said. "You are really fantastic."

"Well, thank you very much. I always try my best when meeting new—"

"You are definitely *in*," I said. "Right, Jonny?"

Jonny stayed quiet about the incredible Darius. What was his problem? Was *he* in or out? I couldn't keep track.

Just then, my cell phone vibrated. I pulled it out and saw that it was our landline at home. I really didn't want to deal with X right now. Couldn't he take care of himself for five minutes? I ignored the call.

"Right," Jonny finally said. "But, dude, you look familiar—"

"Well, I'm glad you like it," Darius said. "You want to play some more? I love to play!" He went back to tuning his snare drum, listening to the vibrations of each tap he made like he was hearing the distant music of aliens. Typical music dork, more concerned about his drums being in tune than about the fact that he had just blown away the band he had audi-tioned for. Something was definitely off about this guy. His glasses were cheap-looking, like something you could buy for two dollars at a toy store. And his bushy eyebrows looked too big and cheesy to be real. But I didn't care. He was the best drummer I'd ever played with, by far.

"I don't know about this guy," Jonny whispered.

"What?" Crackers asked.

"Maybe we should talk about this privately," Jonny said.

Darius the Hilarious got the hint. "It was wonderful playing with you guys," he said. "I'll just hang out in the shop for a few."

"What's wrong with you, Jonny? That guy was fantastic," I said after he'd left.

"I thought he was incredible," said Crackers.

"Well, he's fantastic. He's the best drummer in our school, but that's not the point," said Jonny.

"What is the point, then?" I asked.

"He's not who he says he is," Jonny said.

"He's definitely a little weird, but we're all weird," Crackers said.

"That's not what I meant—"

Just then, we heard a loud crash from the front of the store. I opened the drum room door and ran out, Crackers and Jonny right behind me. A big hulking guy with a baseball cap pulled low over his head was holding Darius up by the shirt collar. Darius's feet were six inches above the ground.

"Put me down, man!" he said. His attacker was about ready to throw Darius against the Vintage Wall, and Don Daddio was not going to let that happen.

"Don't even think about it, fool," said Don, stepping between the two kids and the thirty-grand guitar display. He wagged his finger at the bigger one. "Take a deep breath and walk out the door, bud."

The jerk then dropped Darius on the ground, where the drummer landed with a thud. His glasses and fake nose and eyebrows fell to the floor along with him. He wisely stayed put, leaning against a Fender amp.

"Darren, if you go through with this, you're a dead man," the big one said, then pulled off his cap and turned to face us. It was Jackson Royer, of course. And Darius the Hilarious was Darren—aka Curly Burly—the Raising Cain drummer.

"And, Jonny, we've already talked about this. If you become a Bungle, you'd better watch your back," Jackson said.

He had just put a hit out on one-third, or possibly one-half, of my band.

"Oh, and Beatles Girl, you and Quackers'll back off, too, if you know what's good for you. Raising Cain has owned the battle for two years running, and this year will be no different."

"Move on, Jackson," Don said. "And unless you want to be barred from the battle, and from this store, for the rest of your natural-born life, you'd better seriously reconsider that attitude of yours. Now go."

Jackson looked Don square in the eye for an uncomfortably long moment, took two steps backward, then slipped out the door. I swear I could feel the temperature rise a couple degrees in the store once that snake had slithered away.

"Okay, so what are you doing here?" I asked Darren. "Is this some kind of joke?"

He got up groggily, rubbing his hand on his tailbone. "No, it's not a joke. I really want to be in the band."

"Why?" I said. "You're in Raising Cain."

"I've been trying to get out of that band for a year," he

said. "But Jackson isn't exactly the most approachable guy in the world when it comes to . . . change."

"I can imagine," I said. "But how long did you think it'd take for us to figure out who you actually were?"

"Those fake eyebrows were a dead giveaway," said Crackers.

"Well, none of you guys figured it out until Jackson came in here. Except Jonny, maybe. He knew who I was all along, didn't you, buddy?"

"Yep," Jonny said. "Even if your little costume hadn't been so lame, I would have recognized you by your drumming. Duh."

"You guys know each other?" Crackers asked.

"Dude, we were bandmates. Jonny was the original lead guitarist of Raising Cain."

"What?" I said.

"Yeah. It's true." Jonny shifted and glanced at his feet, looking like he couldn't wait to get out of there.

"I thought you knew," said Crackers. "The entire school knows *that*."

"So that's why you didn't want to be a Bungle?" I asked. "Because you thought we'd be the kind of nightmare band-mates that Jackson was?"

"Ha, fat chance," said Darren. "You guys are obviously nothing like Jackson."

"He was probably worried about violent reprisal," Crackers said.

"I'll talk to Jackson," Jonny said. "I think I can make him understand . . ."

"Good luck with *that* little project," I said. "I thought you were afraid of him."

"I'm not. I just . . . respect him enough to stay away from him."

"But you *were* afraid to perform in public with us because of him, right?"

"Yeah, okay, I guess. But I'm done with that now. It's time for me to get away from Jackson, and for good." Jonny turned to Darren. "But, Darren, you're still in it, all the way. Jackson's not going to just let you leave Raising Cain. You realize that'd be like a declaration of war, don't you?"

"First things first," Darren said. "In an ideal world, with no Raising Cain, no Jackson Royer, would you want me to play drums in your band?"

"Yes," Crackers said.

"It depends," I said. "You remember the first day of school, when you told me The Beatles were lame and that I wasn't allowed to make eye contact with you?"

"Um, yeah. I'm sorry about that," Darren said.

"Because if you're going to be in this band, we're going to have to look each other in the eye once in a while."

"Agreed," he said. "That's not really me anyway. That's just an act I put on for Jackson. But it's over now. I'll deal with him."

"There's still the matter of your beating up all the most helpless kids in the school," Crackers said. Go, Crackers!

"That's over and done with," Darren said. "I promise."

"I'll believe it when I see it," I said.

"Listen, I'll make it up to them. I've already been skimming off the top to give as much money *back* to those kids as possible."

"Tell that to Bumblebee Shoes," I said.

"Who?" said Jonny and Crackers.

"She means Angelo. Angelo Martsch," Darren said.

"Darren, where does all the money go anyway? If you're ripping off like half the fifth grade every single day, it must add up to a lot every week," I said.

"At least a hundred a week, sometimes two," Darren said. "We bought all our equipment with that money."

"And after that? What about all the cash since then?" I asked.

"I honestly don't know," Darren said. "Jackson never lets me keep more than ten bucks a week, max. I have a feeling most of it goes to his older brother."

"Yeah, and he's even meaner than Jackson. I think he actually *makes* Jackson do all this, like as some sort of test," said Jonny.

"That's just an excuse," said Darren. "I'm out. I'm out of Raising Cain. And I'm *in* . . . The Bungles?"

"Yeah!" said Crackers and I.

Jonny was silent, but he wore a faint smile.

"You cool, Jonny?" I asked.

"Yep, I'm cool. Welcome to the band, Darren." He put his hand on Darren's shoulder.

And that was it. The Bungles were complete.

Rock stars need bands. And I finally had a band again.

HALF-PIPE

As I walked back home, I replayed all the events of the last hour in my head. We had a drummer! And our drummer was not a doofus genius who had come out of nowhere. He was the same evil freak who had bullied little kids out of lunch money and tried to intimidate me on the first day of school. But he was trying to turn a corner, change himself, and get away from all the bad forces in his life. Could someone make a change like that overnight, though? Could Darren Miller be trusted?

And just as mind-blowingly, I remembered that Jonny had been a member of Raising Cain. A *founding* member of Raising Cain. Unbelievable. How long had he known Jackson? I wondered. And how hard had it been for him to quit? I had seen firsthand that Jackson didn't exactly take rejection well. That must have been why Jonny had been such a loner and so afraid of commitment: he wasn't just afraid of playing with people again; he must have been really scared about what Jackson would do to him if he did. I remembered the first time I had seen Jackson, the way he had coolly examined the scar on Jonny's lip. Had Jackson been the one to put it there?

The real mystery to me, though, was Jackson himself. I was starting to understand his whole junior-mobster approach, especially if it was really some freaky older brother pulling all the strings. But why was he going out of his way to scare me and our band? Raising Cain was untouchably awesome. As much of a stir as we had raised at the open mic, I still had a grip on reality and I knew we were no match for their power and tightness. Still, why else would he write that scary note to Jonny? Why else would he come all the way over to Don Daddio's just to kick Darren's butt? Why would he care? The thought of it made me . . . proud.

With all these thoughts running through my head, I was back in our neighborhood before I knew it, surrounded by the warehouse buildings that blocked out most of the late-afternoon sun. I'd left the store at about four p.m., so X had been alone for six and a half hours. How much trouble could a nine-year-old cause in six and a half hours?

When I got to our apartment door, I could tell something was wrong right away. I quickly put the key in, and the door opened on its own. It had been pulled closed without locking, which meant that X had left the apartment. And if anything had happened to him . . . it was my fault.

"X?" I called from the doorway. I knew there was no way he was there, but it was worth a shot. "You home?"

Of course he wasn't, though. The questions were, where was he, was he okay, and how much trouble was he going to get me into?

I pulled out my phone, which I had turned to silent back when I thought Darius the Hilarious and Curly Burly were two distinct beings. When I saw that there were seventeen missed calls, I started to panic. Something had to be wrong. And sure enough, as soon as I turned the ringer back on, it started wailing away.

"Hello?" I answered.

"Annabelle, where have you been? Damn it, why haven't you picked up your phone?" There was anger in there, for sure. Shock and disappointment, too. You might think these scolding words had come from one of my parents. But it was Shaky Jake.

"I—I turned my phone off for a while."

"And you left your brother alone!"

"Yeah. I left him alone. Is he all right?"

"Well, he's *going* to be all right, but, no, he's very much *not all right* at the moment. He fell off the half-pipe." So he had gone skating, the little punk.

"What? Is he okay?"

"He broke his wrist. In two places."

"Where is he?"

"In the hospital. I'm on the way to pick you up. Be outside in two minutes."

"Okay."

"Annabelle, I'm really disappointed in you." *Click.*

Ouch. You'd have thought I had personally *thrown* X off that half-pipe.

On the way to the hospital, Jake didn't say a word and wouldn't so much as look at me. I wanted to yell, *Wait! You have never given me the silent treatment and you're not allowed to start now! You're supposed to take my side, no matter what!* But Jake's unsmiling face made it clear that he didn't want to hear a peep out of me.

We entered the hospital, where sad, lonely-looking people sat in the waiting room. The sickly light from the fluorescent bulbs above them made their skin look green. Jake pointed me toward X's room, where he said my parents were waiting, and took a detour to the bathroom. I jogged the rest of the way. When I reached the room, I saw X in a massive cast, elevated by a couple of pillows and fast asleep. He looked so sweet and peaceful resting there, and for the first time I realized what I'd done. I'd been so wrapped up in my band, getting a drummer, getting everything *I* wanted, that I'd forgotten I was still an older sister. I'd forgotten what that meant.

My parents were both there, but they hadn't seen me yet and were in the middle of a tense whispering match.

"I don't know what to do," my dad said. "But I'm leaning toward grounding her till she's sixteen."

"But she's *not* sixteen, that's the point," my mom said. "We've put way too much on her shoulders."

"We asked her to sit on her butt at home for a few hours and take care of her little brother," Dad said. "That doesn't seem like too much to ask."

"It is when we've asked her to do it five weekends in a row."

"Five weekends in a row? Really? You've been counting?"

"She's been counting, and she's been counting correctly."

"Maybe we should send her back with my mother, like we discussed. She obviously isn't adjusting to this move."

"I think *we're* the ones who aren't adjusting to the move. Things have to change. Less time on music, more on the kids. It's as simple as that."

"But I'm not getting enough writing time in as it is. I don't want to lose the little time I do have."

"I'm tired of having to be the one to take care of him all the time!" I said. I really surprised the heck out of both of them. I raised my voice, though I made sure I wasn't loud enough to wake up X. "I'm his sister, not his mother. You guys are supposed to be the parents!"

"Well, Belle, we're not like other families," my dad said back. "We all have to chip in to make it work."

"But you *never* chip in, Dad!"

"Sure I do. Don't I?" He looked up at my mom, but she wouldn't look back at him.

Dad grabbed a corner of X's blanket tightly in his right hand and stared at the wall. At first I thought, insanely, that he had gotten an idea for a new song or a new guitar sound or something; he had that same look, like he was searching for something out in the distance. Then, though, he let go of the blanket, slumped in his chair, and said, "Maybe you're right . . . Maybe you're right." He looked totally defeated.

Then Mom stepped toward me. "I'm just glad you're okay, Belle. You really scared us today."

My plan was to be home way before their gig ended; I hadn't realized they might be worried about me, too.

"Sorry, Mom."

"It's okay," she said, wrapping me up in a hug.

"So you're letting her off the hook, just like that?" my dad said.

"Nick, stop it," said my mom.

"Can I say hi to X?" I asked.

"Sure. Just don't wake him up." By now, my brother's contented snoring had filled the room.

"Does it hurt?" I asked my mom.

"He's on enough painkillers to beach a whale," my dad said.

I approached the bed, took X's hand lightly, trying not to disturb him. My dad was right. That kid wouldn't have woken up if Raising Cain had been practicing in the room.

I got right next to his ear and pressed his palm up to my cheek. "X, I'm sorry," I said. Then I whispered in his ear, covering up with my hands so my parents couldn't hear me. "I'm sorry I screwed up. This is all my fault."

Rock stars can be real idiots sometimes.

I GROUND MYSELF

On Sunday, I found R on IM.

EggMtnRckr: Wait, so youre saying that you stole not one but TWO band members from this Razing Kane guy?

Bassinyrface: I didnt steal anybody. They defected.

EggMtnRckr: Ok, ok, but the big bad bully dude is going to kill you. You are messing up Rule Number One for him!

Bassinyrface: Meh. we shall see. i think the tide is turning toward The Bungles.

EggMtnRckr: all right, well if you want me to come up there and kick some butt i will book me a Greyhound ticket.

Bassinyrface: thanks, r. i will let you know!

EggMtnRckr: The Bungles . . . I'm more and more jealous of yr band name.

Bassinyrface: Awww, thanks!!! But it's no Egg Mountain, now, is it?

EggMtnRckr: I dunno. Most people hear Egg Mtn and theyre like, wha?!?

Bassinyrface: heh. maybe.

EggMtnRckr: so how's x? does he have a cast?

Bassinyrface: no, just a sling on his arm.

EggMtnRckr: painful?

Bassinyrface: Not anymore. He was whacked-out on painkillers for a few days, said some hilarious stuff.

EggMtnRckr: Like what?

Bassinyrface: like, Give me my monkey! Or Pujols is slumping! Other stuff like that.

EggMtnRckr: Ha, nice. Now HE is a Bungle. A kid with a broken wrist saying crazy things like that is definitely a Bungle.

Bassinyrface: Totally.

"*We* should be the ones getting grounded!" my mom said late that night, not knowing I had been on my way to the kitchen for a post-homework snack. "If there's anybody getting punished around here, it should be us."

"What are you talking about?" my dad said, throwing his hands up in frustration. "She agreed to take care of her little brother. She didn't do it. Simple as that."

"Hello, Annabelle," said my mom, seeing me out of the corner of her eye.

"Hi," I said.

"Why don't you come join us, honey?" she said. I sat in a chair at the kitchen table, a few feet from the couch where they were sitting.

X was asleep when I'd decided to get something to munch on. I had known my parents would probably want to have a big talk if they saw me, but I figured, better to get it over with.

They'd been having these annoying arguments about "what to do with Annabelle" for the last twenty-four hours. So I figured they must have finally come to an agreement about what kind of punishment I would get. I figured wrong, though. They were disagreeing more than ever.

"It's *not* as simple as you're making it seem," Mom said to my dad. "We've been putting too much pressure on her—on X, too—for months now. We can't keep making her—"

"Can I say something, please?" I actually raised my hand.

"Yes," they both said eagerly, glad for the chance to push pause on their deadlocked argument.

"I ground myself," I said.

"What do you mean exactly?" my dad said.

"I mean, I'm really sorry for what I did, for leaving X like that. I told you I'd take care of him, and I didn't do it. I ground myself . . . for a week."

My dad raised an eyebrow and looked at my mom. She just shrugged and glanced at the wall.

"Fair?" I asked. Did I deserve it? Maybe, but I didn't really care about whether I deserved it or not.

"Fine," they both said.

"No TV, no DVDs, no talking on the phone," I said. I barely did any of that stuff anyway—I texted, used the laptop to IM people, and listened to my iPod while playing Satomi—but my dad didn't know that, so I deliberately suggested outlawing stuff I really didn't care about losing. "I'll come home after school and do my homework. Then if X needs my help with his, I'll give it to him."

"You'll come home *straight* after school, you'll do your homework, do your chores, and go to bed," my dad said. He seemed to love piling it on, even though he was just saying what I had said in different words. My mom stayed mostly quiet, throwing a sigh in here and there.

"Works for me," I said. "But just one thing . . . can I still have band practices, as long as they're here?" That was the one thing I really cared about, so my whole strategy was to sneak it in at the last minute.

"Yes, Annabelle," my mom said. "You can practice here."

Mission accomplished. One mission, at least.

"Belle," my dad said. "Have you given any more thought to whether or not you want to move back to Brooklyn to live with Abuela?"

"I'm still thinking about it," I said. "But what would happen to X? Would he come with me?"

"X would stay with us," Mom said. "We feel that Abuela might not be able to handle X and you both, especially with the way he's been acting lately."

"But the reason he's acting so crazy is because you guys moved us here in the first place."

"Your abuela is getting older, Belle," Dad said. "You're mature enough that you can take care of yourself and don't need her help as much. X needs his parents."

I tried not to laugh. X would be better off all night on a park bench than he would be being ignored every day by my dad. At least, that's how it seemed to me.

"It would be during the Christmas break," Mom said, looking like she might explode into tears again. She also looked angry, almost, or frustrated. I couldn't tell. "We wouldn't want you to miss any school, so we'd drive you down over the holidays, and you'd stay there."

"I don't know," I said, getting out of there as quickly as I could. "I have to think about it."

☆

Monday morning, Mr. V returned my latest attempt at a "work of art."

Where Do I Go (From Here)?
by Annabelle Cabrera

It wasn't my choice
To come to this town
It started off ugly
And it got me so down
Where do I go from here?

I came here with shorts on
But now I'm wearing sweaters
Some days are bad

But other days are better
Where do I go from here?

Ms. Cabrera,

Now we are getting somewhere! This is what I've been hoping to see from you. You are clearly writing from your own experience, but in a way that is communicating something to others, in a way that lets us in . . .

Still, this is a song, yes? Don't most songs have more than two verses? And where is the chorus?

Mr. V

P.S. And it's a little depressing, this sentiment. Perhaps you should look to Jon Bon Jovi for an example of a more uplifting and inspiring message. ☺

Wow, suddenly Mr. V fancied himself a big-shot producer! Uplifting? Inspiring? Come on, Mr. V! Real rock songs might make you feel great when you're listening to them, but they're usually not *about* feeling great; a lot of times they're about feeling mad, or sad, or just . . . wound up and crazy! Still, he had a point—these lyrics were just lyrics, not a song. Not yet.

The following Wednesday, exactly one month before the battle, was D-Day. As in, Darren Day, the first day that a full-fledged, recent member of Raising Cain and Jackson's mini-mafia would enter my apartment, step on my floors, and play music with *my* band. It had been only seven weeks earlier that Curly Burly had knocked into me in the hall and told me not to make eye contact with him. Now, as the rhythm section of The Bungles, we were going to *have* to make eye contact, and plenty of it, for the band to sound halfway decent.

Darren was the first one to ring the doorbell that day. I had asked Jonny to try to make it to my place a few minutes early, just so I could avoid having to hang out with Darren alone, but Jonny was always at least ten minutes late to practice, and today wasn't any different.

"Hey, Annabelle," he said after I buzzed him up. "What's up?"

"You left your Darius the Hilarious disguise at home this time, huh?" I said, trying to lighten the mood.

"That I did." We wandered into the studio part of the apartment. He pointed to the drums and said, "So . . . is that Shaky Jake's kit?"

"Uh, yeah." It was just part of the furniture to me.

"I can't believe I get to play Shaky Jake's drums. He's amazing."

I threw a suspicious look his way. "I thought you were a metalhead," I said.

"My Benny and Joon T-shirt wouldn't have fit my tough-guy image. I like all kinds of music, though," he said. "You want to play a little before the others get here?"

"Okay." I still wasn't entirely sure about him. He seemed cool, nice, normal. But was this the *real* Darren? Or would the real Darren rather have been strutting around the halls, displaying the latest in heavy metal T-shirt fashion and beating kids up?

I plugged in my bass and started playing my White Stripes–ish riff, and Darren came in right away on drums. About eight bars into it, while I repeated the riff, he turned the beat around very cleverly, single-handedly creating a second section of the song where only one had existed before. A truly great drummer can do that kind of thing, actually take part in writing a song by doing smart things with the beat. I stopped thinking about the real Darren, distracted by the fact that we were making some real *music*. I didn't have to give him any suggestions; he knew exactly where I was going, predicting when I would get louder, when I would go from the verse to the chorus, when the song was about to hit its climax. It was all second nature to him. With this guy on drums, The Bungles were going to be amazing.

The doorbell rang again before we were finished.

"Cool riff," Darren said.

"Thanks." I walked toward the front door to buzz in Jonny and Christine, who arrived together.

"You written any lyrics for that one yet?" Darren asked.

"Nope," I replied.

"Has Christine?"

"She doesn't write songs."

"Yet." He laughed, while I thought, *Grrr.*

After Jonny and Christine came up, we didn't talk much before getting down to business.

"What would you guys think about doing two covers and one original at the battle?" I asked.

"Works for me," said Jonny. "Which of your songs do you wanna do?"

"It's a new one," I said. The first genuine, fully fleshed-out result of the Mr. V assignment. School was good for something, after all.

"Okay," said Crackers, nodding.

"Cool," said Jonny.

"Fine by me," said Darren. "If I get a vote yet, that is." That got a laugh.

"Which covers?" asked Jonny.

"Well, I was thinking we could do 'A Place in the Sun' so Christine can belt one out, and then maybe 'Basket Ball Get Your Groove Back,' by Deerhoof."

It's an amazing song that features Satomi chanting phrases like "B ball, B ball, B ball" and "rebound" and "bunny jump, bunny jump" over and over again against counterrhythms in the guitar and drums. It was easily my favorite track off their last album, and I really wanted to try it with the band.

"That's a tough song, Annabelle," said Jonny. "I don't know."

"Never heard of it," said Crackers.

"Well, I know the lyrics and the bass line," I said.

"I can play that one," said Darren. So he wasn't kidding. He did listen to a lot of different stuff.

"Yeah, but . . . I don't know how well that one'll go over in the battle," Jonny said. "It's a little out there."

Again, *Grrr.*

"Well, how about we try it out today, and if it's not working, we can pick something else," I said.

"Okay," said Jonny.

We played a couple easy songs, and with Darren even these simple tunes sounded amazing. We sounded like— A. Rock. Band. And a really good one, too. Then Darren and I started playing the Deerhoof song. Darren sounded great, of course. The beat was solid but always evolving; you couldn't help but glue your ears to it. But as soon as I came in, singing and playing bass, it was a train wreck.

"Hold on one sec," I said. "I'll get it."

I had practiced this thing pretty much straight for the last three days with my iPod, but even in this low-pressure situation, I gagged. I simply did not have it together.

"Okay, that was a disaster," I said.

"Let's play a Strokes song," said Jonny, always the diplomat.

"Let's break for a snack," Crackers said.

"Sweet," said Darren. "I'm starving."

We went to the kitchen and made some sandwiches, during which Jonny and Darren started reminiscing about their hellish tenure with Raising Cain. According to Jonny, one of the major issues was that Darren drove Jackson crazy with his constant chatting, blathering on and on about nothing in particular.

"I thought you were the strong, silent type," I said to Darren.

"Strong, maybe. Silent? Not so much," Jonny said.

"Jackson used to fine me for talking in rehearsals," Darren said.

"Seriously?" Crackers said.

"Dude was ultra-serious about music. He kept tabs on everything."

"Five bucks for every 'infraction,'" Jonny said.

"I owe him a couple hundred bucks!" Darren laughed. "Do I still have to pay him, now that I'm not even in his band?"

And there was no stopping Darren after that. Now that he knew there'd be no financial consequences for his spastic, motormouth conversational approach, he was a new man. Or man-boy, or whatever. He was a true force of nature, offering ideas and opinions, jokes and observations on every subject under the sun. And he somehow did this without getting on my nerves. A miracle. There were other surprising things about Darren, too. Every time we had a snack, he'd get up right after he was done and would clear *and wash* all the dishes before anybody else had a chance. When Darren called my parents Mr. and Mrs. Cabrera, Crackers and I started calling him Boy Scout. He even tried to put a "Mr." in front of Shaky Jake, before Jake corrected him.

"I've never been a mister in my life, and I'm not about to start now," Jake said.

I also couldn't help but notice that Darren had nice chestnut eyes and forearms that were strong and tight from all that drumming, and I thought, *Oh no you don't. He might be cute, but he's a Bungle now, not just some random eighth grader. Hands off. Mind off. Everything off.*

THREE GOOD WEEKS

On Monday, I handed in my song to the V Man.

Mr. V,

Okay, this is getting there!

Where Do I Go (From Here)?
by Annabelle Cabrera

It wasn't my choice
To come to this town
It started off ugly
And it got me so down
Where do I go from here?

I came here with shorts on
But now I'm wearing sweaters
Some days are bad
But other days are better
Where do I go from here?

I want to break out,
I want to be free,
I want you to be you,
And me to be me
But where do I go from here?

Some people don't seem to know anything
Don't want me to rock, don't want me to sing
So where do I go from here?

P.S. Actually, not all songs have to have a chorus. I know
you said you'd die a happy man if you never have to hear
"Hey Jude" again, but I happen to think "Hey Jude" is
pretty great—I think you'd find a lot of people who agree
with me on this—and it doesn't have a chorus.

☆

Wednesday, eight a.m., precisely three weeks before the battle. While I eavesdropped from my personal area, my parents
were in the kitchen arguing. Again.

"Because I'm not sure if I *want* to tour behind this record,"
my mom said.

This was rare. The fighting between my parents had been

getting worse and worse since X's accident, but usually they kept up appearances in front of us. The family meeting, the one where they'd fought about grounding me, was the first time I'd seen them openly argue in front of me. But that had only been preparation for battle. Now they were in a flat-out war.

"We *have* to tour if we want to sell more than three copies of this thing," countered my dad.

"Yeah? Who's going to take care of the kids?"

"I've said this a dozen times already," he said with obvious impatience. "We'll send them *both* down to Brooklyn. Then, when the tour's over, we'll bring X back here."

Ha! That was just not going to happen. My dad was grasping at straws.

"There is no way we can just rip him out of school like that. We are being terrible parents! Can't you see it?"

Whoa. She had never said anything like *that* before. This was serious.

"Okay, okay, take it easy," my dad said. He knew she had him. I could almost see him holding up his hands in defeat. "We'll work it out."

After that argument, though, for the two weeks leading up to the battle, the gloves were off. They argued about anything and everything: laundry, food, practice schedules, album art. There was no subject, large or small, that went without comment. Where before Mom would let Dad take the lead on everything, whether he was right or wrong, now she wouldn't let him get away with anything. She had him backed into a corner, and I had never seen him so off his game. When he tried to help her cut up some carrots for X's lunch—he had probably never made lunch for X or me in our entire lives—I thought she was going to chop his finger off.

On the other hand, my mom, X, and I were getting along great. Since X's accident, she and I had had to help him with a whole mess of super-basic tasks, anything from writing out his homework to getting dressed. For the first two weeks, there actually wasn't much he *could* do by himself. The kid couldn't even tie his own shoelaces.

"It's like he's a doll and we're playing dress-up," I said one morning as I was buttoning his shirt.

"I am *not* a doll," X said, but I could tell he didn't mind. He loved being fussed over.

"We could tie his shoelaces together, and there's not a thing in the world he could do about it," my mom said.

"Better not!" said X, laughing and pulling his feet away.

Maybe breaking his wrist had been a stroke of genius. He had been screaming for attention, and now he was getting more of it than he knew what to do with. The three of us were spending more time together than ever before; even in Brooklyn, I had never hung out with my mom this much. My dad would stay up in the loft, reading or listening to music, while Mom, X, and I felt like an actual family.

For the first time in a while, just about everything was going well for me. X and I were getting along, my band was an actual band, and I couldn't wait for the battle. It was the best three weeks I'd had since we'd moved to Providence.

THE BASS GODDESS
AND THE BULLY

One week before the battle. It was Friday the thirteenth. Spooky.

Mr. V motioned me over to his desk as soon as I walked into his classroom.

"Ms. Cabrera, come here for a moment, please," he said. When I approached his desk, and he held his hand out to me formally, as if we were meeting for the first time, I cracked up. "I want to congratulate you on your work of art."

I stopped my giggling. "My . . . what do you mean? My song?"

"I very much enjoyed 'Where Do I Go (From Here)?' I think it's remarkable work and I'd like to read it aloud in today's class. Do you mind?"

"Umm, I don't know. I . . ." The bell rang.

"I'll take that as a yes," he said, and before I could think better of it he was standing in front of the class with my song in his hand.

"Students, I have been trying to make writers of you this year," he said. "I started with a cheap ploy, really, letting the great Bon Jovi do my work for me. Who wouldn't have been inspired?" A chuckle from McNamara, that clown in the back row. "Many of you have risen to the task. You have used the songs to delve into memories; you have described events in your life with a keen eye. But few of you have managed to crack the shell of your emotional lives"—at this, I sank in my chair—"to *reveal* something of yourselves in your work.

"The following song—it also succeeds very much as a freestanding poem—does just that. Please listen."

Then he recited my song from start to finish. I could feel Crackers's eyes on me—we had been practicing this one for the last three weeks, so of course she recognized it from the first line. She gave me a quick smile, but I just looked down and squeezed the top of my desk with both hands, praying for him to get to the end without my identity being revealed. I *hated* hearing my song read aloud. The lyrics sounded terrible without music—so personal and cheesy! So *un*rock! I felt like he was reading my diary to the entire class, without any loud guitars and drums to bury the lyrics. But the class listened in respectful silence, and I was starting to think I would survive.

Mr. V surveyed the class. "Well, any comments on this work?"

"I thought it was great," said Christine. "The words are

good, and the feelings are real." Whew. She had obviously figured out from my body language that I wanted to stay anonymous.

"Yeah," another kid said. "It was cool."

But then McNamara piped in. "Nice work, Annabelle," he said sarcastically. "That was totally . . . moving." His goon buddies cracked up.

"Mr. McNamara, do you have anything sincere to add to this conversation?" Mr. V said, silencing everyone. "Because if you want, I could read your essay on your grandmother. The one in which you compare her clear blue eyes to a lovely summer sky?" Silence. "Good choice. It needs work."

"Well, I hadn't intended on revealing the author," he continued. "But now that you know, I think Ms. Cabrera has done a wonderful job here. The writing is concise and direct. The emotions are tangible and real. My compliments." He handed the sheet back to me, with a massive A written at the top in blue ink. "Oh, and good luck to you and Christine at the battle of the bands."

I should have skipped all the way back to my locker, high on my second A in a row, but something bothered me: I didn't think the song was any good. Even if Mr. V thought it was "emotionally revealing" or whatever, it just felt off to me. And there was no way I could perform it in public if the words didn't feel right. I'd have to keep working on it.

Darren found me at my locker.

"Yo, Belle," he said.

"What's up?" I turned around to find him wearing a sling on his right arm.

"You've got to be kidding me," I said. The battle was a week away.

"I wish I was," he said. "I broke my elbow."

"What happened?"

"Jackson happened."

"Jackson broke your elbow?"

"Well, not exactly. But the guy who did it was definitely, um . . . employed by Jackson."

"Okay . . ."

"He introduced himself as Raising Cain's new drummer. He looked about thirty years old. And he was huge. Two hundred pounds of pure muscle."

"What'd he do?"

"He sucker-punched me as I was walking home yesterday. Then he pushed me over, and I guess I must have broken my fall with my elbow."

"Ouch."

"You're telling me. It kills."

"Darren, I'm really sorry."

"It's okay. I can still play."

"Are you crazy? That's your right hand. You're a *right-handed* drummer. There's no way you can play."

"Haven't you ever heard of Def Leppard? That drummer lost, like, three limbs in a drunken car accident, and he can still rock out."

"I wasn't aware of that."

"Seriously, I need to do this. For me. To show Jackson that

he and his goons can't keep me down. He'll have to break both legs to keep me off that stage."

"Shh," I said. I didn't point out that only three weeks ago he had been one of those goons. "Don't give him any ideas."

☆

The day before the battle.

"Belle, sweetheart, I need to talk to you about something," my mom said as I was making my lunch in the kitchen.

"What?" I looked around. "What's going on?"

"Nothing, sweetie. Everything's fine." She nervously tapped her fingers on the countertop.

"Mom, what's wrong? Is X okay? Is everything okay?"

"Yes, yes." She nervously brushed back her hair. "It's just that . . . Well, Belle, you know how your dad and I, we need to perform to keep bread on the table . . ."

"Okay . . ." As if I hadn't heard this speech a million times.

"See, Benny and Joon got a great offer to play in Boston, and it's . . . Well, it's tomorrow."

"The night of the battle? You're not going to make it to the battle?" I took the knife I was using to spread peanut butter and threw it in the sink. Then I started pacing around the room. I admit that I probably looked fairly crazy at this moment in time. But I was mad.

"Belle, I know. Believe me, I know. But just listen. We'll be playing at the Somerville Theatre. It's a pretty big venue. And we'll open for PJ Harvey. You know how much this means to your dad. She's one of his favorite—"

I stopped pacing and gave my mom a look that stopped her in her tracks.

"I get it, Mom. It's back to the way things were."

"Don't, Belle—"

"I know how things work in this family. Dad comes first. He always has and he always will."

Then I marched into the bathroom. Remember, that was the only slammable door in the place.

"Belle, that's not fair." Mom followed me. "Come on, open up."

I vowed to never open up. Not in a million years. Or at least not until I could escape from the house without having to talk to my mom again.

While my temples pounded with rage, I thought again about what Mr. V had said about how craziness is defined as doing the same thing or seeing the same thing again and again and expecting something different to happen. But I think the definition of craziness is living with my mom. I mean, for my whole life *she* had done the same thing over and over again, which was to side with my dad. On literally everything. And then, starting at the hospital, she seemed to start siding with X and me. She had seen how my dad's way of doing things wasn't working, so she was moving away from him and toward us. But how did that explain her ditching me on the most important night of my life for a PJ Harvey opening slot that hadn't even existed twenty-four hours ago? Who was crazy: my mom, or me?

"Belle," Mom said, still outside the door. "Please open up, sweetie. Come on."

"I'm fine, Mom," I said. "I'm just going to take a shower. I'm not mad anymore." Ha, what a lie.

I did get in the shower and think things over. Logically, it shouldn't have been that annoying to me for my mom not to come to the battle. She hadn't been to the open mic, and that had gone fine. She hadn't seen me play in Central Park—they'd had a gig in some rock toilet in Philadelphia the same night—and that had been *amazing*. She hadn't even come to my fifth-grade graduation—Abuela had. Why should the last three weeks have made a difference? My mom wasn't going to change. She would always put Benny and Joon ahead of me. She would always put my dad in front of the rest of the family, so it was stupid to expect anything different.

After I dried off, I waited to make sure my mom wasn't by the door anymore and got dressed as quickly as I could. I walked to the front door and carefully unlatched the lock.

That's when I felt two quick taps on my shoulder. I turned around and saw X.

"Belle, I—"

"X, I can't hang out with you right now. I've gotta go to school."

"Belle, I got something for you," X whispered.

"What?"

"It's for good luck," he said. "At the battle."

He held out a little plastic bag filled with guitar picks, the kind of big, wide picks that I liked.

"You bought me picks?"

"Special picks."

I opened up the bag and spilled a few out into my hand.

On one side, they said "Annabelle Cabrera" in big letters. On the other, they said, "Bass Goddess!"

"X, where'd you get these?" I asked. "How'd you pay for them?"

"Don ordered them for me. He said I can work them off, once my arm gets better."

I leaned down on one knee and gave X a hug, careful not to mess with his bad arm.

"Thanks, X," I said, although other than that I was speechless. What can you say when the little brother whose arm you basically broke in two turned around and gave you one hundred customized guitar picks? I gave him a peck on the cheek, then bolted.

Rock stars aren't half as cool as little brothers.

☆

Twenty-four hours before the battle.

I decided not to go home after school. I talked to Crackers and Jonny and convinced them we needed to rehearse. Jonny offered his place, and that would definitely beat going home. Home meant Benny and Joon rehearsing for the big show and my dad going on and on about how he was finally going to meet the great PJ Harvey.

I met Crackers in front of her math class and we walked together to meet Jonny down the hall. But we couldn't find him. Instead, Bumblebee Shoes was there, sitting in front of Jonny's locker, his hair mussed yet again, his T-shirt ripped at the collar. He wasn't crying this time. I guess he was beyond that. He stared straight ahead across the hall and wiped a slow trickle of blood from his nose.

"Angelo, what happened?" I asked.

"Take a wild guess."

"Not again! I'm gonna kill him. Where is he?"

"Who, your friend?" he said bitterly. He wouldn't even look up. "He just went around the corner to chase down a couple other kids."

I turned to Christine. "Darren."

"There's no way he'd go back on his word," Crackers said. "Plus, he's got a broken elbow!"

"Right. Maybe it's Jackson, then. I don't know. Let's just go."

"What? Are you nuts? Don't do this, Annabelle. You'll regret it."

We didn't have to look far. As soon as we started jogging to where Angelo had pointed, we saw a big hulk of a boy who had hold of two kids in Angelo's weight class. He held them by their shirt collars about two inches off the ground while they rifled through their pockets for any loose change they had. I didn't waste any time.

"Hey you, let those guys go. Right! Now!" I yelled from the end of the hall.

He did, and the kids stood frozen on the spot. But even before this big punk turned around, I had a sinking feeling in my stomach. I saw his profile, and he didn't have Jackson's scraggly goatee *or* Darren's curly hair. What he did have was a very familiar mop of messy hair and a big black puffy jacket.

Jonny turned around with a look of pure sorrow on his face.

"Jonny, what the hell do you think you're doing?" I blurted out.

"You're . . . with Raising Cain again? You're, like, in the Federal Hill mafia?" Crackers said.

As soon as they saw Jonny was distracted, the two kids ran off.

"It's not what it looks like, okay?" Jonny said.

"What, these shrimps owe you for Girl Scout cookies? You're a jerk!" I said.

"Shut up, Annabelle! You don't know anything about me!" His voice was a throaty rasp. "You don't know anything at all."

Jonny sprinted away, dropping his backpack and a bunch of cash and change as he went. Christine and I ran after him. He kicked open the doors that led to the playground, then beelined it toward the gate that led to the street outside. I couldn't keep up with him, but I saw him head toward the swing set. Jonny tried to jump one of the swings, but he got tangled up in the chain and hit the ground with a thud. He clutched his left shin, rocking back and forth, and I could hear him huffing and puffing from halfway across the yard. I slowed down as I got closer to him, afraid he might erupt again. But he just lay there, nursing his wound and rocking himself on the black rubber jigsaw mat under the swings.

He looked at me out of the corner of his eye. "I never wanted to hurt those kids," he said. "They used to be my friends."

"Why'd you do it, then?"

"You see this?" he said, pointing to the scar on his lip. "Jackson said he'd give me another one to match it."

"Yeah? I thought you were going to 'talk to him.' You said you'd figure it out."

"I did. I tried. I really thought I'd be able to talk to him about all this. I mean, he and I were best friends for four years. But he wouldn't budge. He said that if Darren quit getting the money, I'd have to do it in his place—or else. And I'm not like Darren. I'm not tough enough to laugh off a smashed hand or a broken cheekbone."

"So it was either shake down those kids or he'd beat the hell out of you?"

"Yep. He also said if I kept playing with The Bungles, he'd personally make sure I'd never be able to pick up a guitar again."

"Well, that sucks. But it doesn't make it okay," I said.

"You could have told a teacher," said Crackers.

"Yeah, right," Jonny said. "You know what Jackson would have done to me if I had gotten him busted? I'd be talking to you from a hospital bed right now."

"You could have told *us*," I said.

He couldn't come up with an answer to that one.

"Just how long has this been going on?" said Crackers.

Again, Jonny said nothing. He just looked down at the ground.

"It's been him all year," I said, finally realizing it. "He's been bullying these kids for their money, just like the rest of Raising Cain."

We walked away.

"Guys, come on. Wait up," he said. But we kept walking, and we didn't talk until we were out the door.

"What do we do now?" Crackers said.

"We figure out how we're going to compete in the battle with half a drummer. And without a guitar player at all."

NO SLO-MO

Two hours before the battle.

I went over it a hundred times in my head. I talked it over with Jake at home that afternoon and obsessed about it with Crackers on the phone. But each time I came to the same conclusion: The Bungles would have to withdraw from the battle. Crackers and I were both still too mad at Jonny to play with him anytime soon, but we couldn't play without him, either. His guitar parts were too important, and there was no way someone else could learn them in time. Jackson had achieved his goal. The Bungles were out of the battle. The Bungles weren't even a band.

I got to Don Daddio's at about three thirty. All day I had told myself I wouldn't go there, but in the end I couldn't help myself. I was a sucker for punishment. Not only was I going to allow Jackson to break up my band, I was going to watch

Raising Cain win it all. Just as I crossed the threshold to the shop, my pocket buzzed. It was a text from Ronaldo.

"With Abuela right now," it read. "She says to make her proud tonight. Same from me. You are an official MASTER OF THE RULES!!!"

Excellent. I was going to make them so proud! Instead of staying at home like anybody with self-respect would, I was going to watch Raising Cain win. I was going to be a bystander to my own humiliation.

Don had done an impressive job setting up. He had made the small parking lot behind the shop look like a real rock club. It was the last Friday before Thanksgiving, so there was a serious chill in the air, and the sun was already low in the sky. The stage was an intimidating five feet off the ground. Behind it a banner read "Minor Threat Battle of the Bands" in massive letters. There were about a hundred folding chairs in the lot, and a sound guy with a pink and green Mohawk worked buttons and levers behind an enormous soundboard. He flicked a switch and a whole rainbow of spotlights came on, circling in crisscross patterns across the stage.

"You playing tonight, hon?" asked the sound guy.

"Um, no," I said. "Not tonight."

"I beg to differ," said a voice behind me. I turned around to see Don, smiling behind me. "This is Annabelle Cabrera. Her band, The Bungles, will indeed be performing tonight."

"No, we won't, Don. I came here to tell you."

"You come with me, young lady." He walked a few feet toward the stage and pulled out two of the folding chairs. "We need to have us a little chat."

As I sat down, I felt my face turning red. I had never seen Don so serious. He was really glaring at me.

"Your nephew was doing Jackson's dirty work," I said. "Beating up kids and taking their money for no good reason."

"I know all about it. I've known Jonny since the day he was born. And I certainly know more about this situation than you do."

"Why are you talking to me like this? I didn't do anything wrong."

"You've turned your back on a friend."

"But Jonny lied to me. He's been lying for months."

"Well, it's been a complicated situation for him. Jackson has been bullying him for a very, very long time."

"What difference—"

"Since the second grade, in fact. We've tried to get the school involved. Once, even the cops. But Jackson has his hooks in Jonny, somehow. It's like he's got a power over the kid."

"That's very touching," I said. Don just ignored me and kept going.

"But don't confuse them. Not for a second. Jackson is just a bad kid. Jonny, however, is not. He's scared maybe, and he's made some bad decisions because of it."

"So that's supposed to make it all okay? Jonny's life's not a bowl of cherries, so he gets forgiven? For everything?"

"Have you ever been bullied, Belle? Repeatedly, consistently, over several years?"

I didn't nod. I didn't shake my head. I just sat there.

"Right. I didn't think so. Listen, I know your life hasn't exactly been perfect lately, either, but bullying's no joke. I think you should cut Jonny some slack."

"Okay, okay. Jeez."

Don scratched his head and chuckled under his breath. "Sorry, Belle. I'm coming on a little strong, huh? Listen, I'm not asking you to *forgive* Jonny, at least not right away. I'm just asking you to understand him. And I'm hoping you'll play tonight. The Bungles are still on the set list. Jonny's coming, and so's the rest of your band. I've made sure of that. As to whether you perform or not, well, that'll be your choice, of course. Yours and your bandmates'. Just keep me posted on what you decide."

"Don, I didn't even bring Satomi. I don't even have a bass."

"Oh, I guess you can't play, then. Not when there are forty basses ten feet away, any of which you'd be welcome to use tonight. The Beatle bass, for example."

The Hofner! The man knew me well.

☆

If this had been a movie, Jonny would have entered the store in slo-mo. He and I would have met dead center in the middle of the store and exchanged meaningful looks without speaking a single word. Tears would have sat in our eyelids, waiting to stream down as we hugged and jabbered on about forgiveness and gratitude and life lessons and how much we cared about each other. Cue the cheesy music, the violins.

But of course it didn't happen that way. Jonny, Crackers, and Darren arrived at Don's together, which really annoyed me; they had obviously been talking behind my back. And then they walked by me *without even seeing me.* Granted, Don's was buzzing with people, and I wasn't exactly keeping a high profile; I had my hood up and was skulking around like a juvenile delinquent.

My bandmates, or former bandmates, or whatever they were, stopped by the counter to strategize. I knelt behind a Marshall stack and listened.

"Just how mad was she the last time you talked to her?" Darren asked Crackers.

"I don't know if she's really even mad anymore," Crackers said. Yes, I was! "She seems more—I don't know—sad."

"What do you think'll make her sadder?" Darren asked. "Realizing that Jonny's not Mr. Perfect or missing out on this battle, which she's been working on for over two months?"

"Excuse me, Darren," Crackers said. "It's more than just Jonny not being Mr. Perfect. He's been a total jerk. And you have, too. Do I need to remind you?" *Gooooo* Crackers! I had never seen her get this riled up before.

"Okay, okay," Jonny said, finally breaking his silence. "Darren and I have both screwed things up pretty badly. He knows it; I know it. But we agreed that, for now at least, we are going to try to patch things up, right?" He looked at Christine, raising his eyebrows. "That we've worked too hard to quit now? That we'll play the battle, and then sort things out afterward?"

"Yeah," Crackers said grudgingly. "That's what we said."

I stepped out from behind the amp.

"Do I get a say in this?" I asked.

"Well, yeah," Darren said. "Obviously."

I turned and faced Jonny. "I just want to know," I said. "Why did you lie to me? Why did you keep screwing with those kids even after you said you were breaking all ties with Jackson?"

"I . . . I tried," Jonny said. "But the first time I didn't bring my weekly totals, he jumped me on Waterman Street, after all. He said he'd *kill* me if I stopped or if I told anybody. He looked crazy—crazier than I'd ever seen him before. So I didn't know what to do. I just kept doing what I'd been doing all year."

"But it's over now?"

"Well, I mean now that Jackson knows that *Don* knows the whole story, I think I'm cool. I think Jackson's going to back off. At least for a while."

Darren reached out and put his good hand on Jonny's shoulder, just for a split second, before pulling it back.

"Will you play with us, Belle?" Darren asked. "I think we owe it to ourselves to play tonight."

"Darren, you've got a broken elbow," I said. "Can you even play?"

"The guy in Def Leppard has like one limb, and he sounds great," Jonny said. "I think Darren can manage."

"Enough about Def Leppard!" I said. "Let's do it. But once we get off that stage, we're all going to talk about a way for you two to make it up to those kids."

"Okay," Jonny said.

"And it's got to be something good," I said. "Not just some lame apology. You've got to make it up to them for real."

"You guys can be their personal slaves for the next three years," Crackers said.

Jonny chuckled awkwardly.

"No joke," I said, but I could tell he was taking it very, very seriously.

So that was that. For the day at least, we were still a band. All the bandmates (with the possible exception of Darren) were mad and unbelievably tense, but we were still a band.

☆

At four fifteen, when we got called up for a sound check, we were still communicating in nods and grunts. We climbed the stage by some stairs on the side and started setting up our instruments. The rainbow of lights came on. "Whoa!" said Crackers, and I realized she had never been on a real stage before. As I was fiddling with the house amp—that night everybody was using the same amps and the same drum set—I saw Jackson arrive. He was wearing shades and a knit cap. Either he didn't want to be seen just yet or he was trying out a completely unsuccessful new look. I don't think he realized I had spotted him, but he looked as cocky as ever. He approached the Mohawk sound guy and gave him a big cool-dude handshake, like they had known each other for years. Then he whispered something in the guy's ear.

"Annabelle, you ready?" said Crackers. "We only have five minutes. Let's try a song."

"Check, check," I said into the mic. Crackers did the same. "You ready for us?"

"Um, yeah. Go for it," said the sound guy, who couldn't stop smirking for some reason. "Play something."

Darren did a quick count-off and we started "Is This It," the Strokes song—we hadn't had time to decide what our set list was going to be yet, but we could figure that out before the actual performance. Jonny and I still weren't making eye contact, but there was still a nice bounce to our playing. The Bungles didn't sound like anybody else, and the fact that we weren't all best-friend cuddly at the moment didn't change that. Maybe we'd be like Oasis or the Pixies, I thought, one of those bands where everybody wants to kill each other half the time, but they sound amazing anyway. By the end of "Is This It," we still weren't exactly having a love fest onstage. I was angry; maybe *all* of us were a little angry, but the anger was helping us play better, stronger, tighter. As we played the last chord, we didn't want to let the next band do their sound check. We wanted to keep playing.

"When do you think Don'll kick us off?" Darren asked.

"Whatever," Jonny joked. "I'm not goin' anywhere."

"Oh my God," I said. "That's it!"

I almost threw my guitar down, rushing to get the pad and paper from my backpack.

"Whoa, Cabrera, what's the rush?" Jonny asked.

"Sorry," I said. "I've got to get some lyrics down. I think I might have finally figured out how to finish my song!"

"You go, girl," Jonny said as I scribbled words down so fast that to anyone else but me it would have looked like some strange Martian language.

Rock stars don't get mad. They write songs.

The Bungles' Children's Choir

By seven o'clock, the chairs were starting to fill up, and not just with Federal Hill people, either. A lot of hipster-type college kids and art students came, all mopey-looking bangs and eyeliner. And most of the guitar geeks I saw every time I showed up at Don's were there, some of them practicing licks on invisible guitars while they waited in their seats. The revamped formation of Raising Cain sprawled on a few chairs to the side of the stage. Cory, the new drummer, might not have been as old as Darren had described him, but he was definitely massive. He was dressed head to toe in denim and leather, with mutton chops that met at his chin. Jackson looked as relaxed and above it all as usual, lounging about as if he expected a lowly servant to sidle up at any moment to pop a couple of grapes into his mouth.

Don Daddio took the stage.

"All right, rockers, who's ready to get down to business?" Mild cheers from the audience. "Who's ready to tear the roof off and kick out the jams?" The cheers were getting louder, but they were still pretty weak. "People, this isn't some indie rock show where you show your appreciation by sitting on your hands and crying into your beer. This is a battle of the bands! Who's ready to WAGE SOME WAR?" A real cheer this time, some screams. "This is the Sixth Annual Minor Threat Battle of the Bands! Remember, you're the voters, and you're going to vote with DECIBELS. The trophy goes to the band that gets the rowdiest ruckus, so lemme hear you make some noise!"

This time, the audience stood up and really screamed. Don Daddio turned back on one heel and smiled as he watched the crowd go absolutely nuts. A bunch of boys from the back started chanting "Raising Cain, Raising Cain" at the top of their lungs.

"Good segue, people, because as last year's champs, Raising Cain is going to kick things off for us tonight with a three-song set of their pulverizing brand of take-no-prisoners rawwwwk 'n' rollllll. Let's give a hand to Jackson and the boys!"

The crowd roared in approval as Raising Cain sauntered onto the stage with a lazy confidence. At least half of their magic came from the fact that they looked like they just didn't care. The bassist plugged in a black Music Man bass with an MDC sticker on it. Jake had told me about them. The initials stood for Millions of Dead Cops, or possibly Multi-Death Corporation depending on who you asked, but either way it was creepy and weird. Cory looked half asleep and droopy eyed, but warmed up with lightning-fast fills on his snare drum and tom-toms. And Jackson strutted around on the stage, twisting the mic cord in his hand like a whip he was about to uncoil on the audience. The crowd murmured expectantly.

Finally, Jackson put his guitar strap over his shoulder, plugged into a vintage Marshall combo amp, and kicked off the vicious first number of their set, "Raw Power," another Stooges song. The band sounded absolutely awesome. The bassist and the drummer were totally locked in as Jackson's sneering vocals and crunchy guitar leads pierced the air. It was an aggressive, rude sound played with clarity and precision. Raising Cain took petty cruelty and turned it into art. Everyone in the audience was on their feet throughout the song, and when it ended, they erupted.

Jackson put his hand out to quiet the crowd, tuned his guitar for a moment, and approached the microphone. "Thanks so much, everyone, for giving us the chance to shine on." His voice sounded as greasy and slick as the goop he used to plaster down his hair. "It feels good to kick it out a little . . . So, for the next two songs, I've got some dedications. This first one goes out to all the . . . well, all the little people at Federal Hill. They have been supporting me, literally, all year, and it's been a pleasure to make so many new friends. It's truly a humbling thing to be part of a community."

Man, I thought, *the guy is really pushing it to the limit.*

"Okay, sorry to get all mushy. This is a Slayer tune. They are the godfathers of speed metal. We now pay homage with our modest and lowly version of 'Mind Control.'"

How many synonyms for "humble" does Jackson Royer know? I thought. How like Jackson to play the politician—he really did sound like a candidate for something, with all the fake claims to modesty—and then toast his scrawny victims with a twisted anthem about bullying and torture.

Still, I couldn't deny Raising Cain's power. You'd have to be deaf to say they were anything but terrifyingly great. Jackson's guitar rose above the tight interplay of bass and drums, cutting into the crowd like a knife. And his deep, rumbling speaking voice transformed onstage into the bark and growl of a true metal screamer. The audience was in a kind of trance. They banged their heads in time like ancient worshipers. When the music stopped, they howled yet again.

"Okay, folks, it's been fun," Jackson said. "We've got just one more for you, and this one I'd like to dedicate to a girl who's a fledgling rocker herself." His voice was as sweet as syrup, and he faked an innocent smile that stretched tightly across his face. "She's a major Beatles fan, so I thought we'd do a little Paul McCartney tune for her." His tone of voice wasn't fooling anybody. He made it clear he hated my guts. "Her band's playing later, so all the luck in the world to little Annabelle Cabrera!"

Jackson turned his back to the crowd and tuned up, tossing his head back and arching his spine like a panther. The Raising Cain guys were at the ready—they looked like chained dogs, frothing at the mouth and set to spring on the next passerby. Then they lit into an unbelievably heavy version of "Helter Skelter," probably the hardest-rocking thing Paul had ever written. I had always liked the song, but I was almost afraid of it, too. It wasn't the Paul of "Blackbird" and "I Want to Hold Your Hand." In "Helter Skelter," The Beatles sound like absolute maniacs. I had never really understood the lyrics before, but today, listening to the words, listening to Jackson's dominating voice, I got the idea.

Superiority, destruction, control. Who knows what Paul McCartney meant when he wrote the song, but Raising Cain made it sound like a declaration of war. Leave it to Jackson Royer to take the thing I loved most in the world and turn it against me.

Raising Cain wasn't just a very good band. They were an impossibly *great* band, especially for three kids who were just eighth graders. They sounded as good as the bands they covered, and the crowd let them know it. It was all Don could do to get the audience to calm down long enough for him to thank Raising Cain and invite the next band to start setting up.

Darren put his hand—the one connected to his one fully working arm—on my shoulder. "They suck, huh?" he said. It was the first time Darren ever touched me. Yikes.

"Totally," I said with a weak smile.

Crackers looked awestruck by Raising Cain's awesomeness, and Jonny was looking at his toes. *The Bungles,* I thought to myself. *What a perfect name for this band. We are going to get laughed off the stage.*

After two quick months of practice, there was no way our band could even come close to being as tight, as fierce, as overpowering as the band we'd just seen. I was four foot ten, Crackers was a snack addict, our drummer had one arm, and our guitar player was an emotional wreck. After just one performance, Minor Threat may as well have been over. Raising Cain would win, hands down. They'd come to Federal Hill tomorrow and be treated like heroes. And Jackson Royer would keep on exploiting all the kids who couldn't fight back.

☆

The next three bands were a joke: underrehearsed, unpolished, and lacking in any talent whatsoever. Even worse, they were attempting to turn Top 40 music into rock 'n' roll. Try as hard as they could, they couldn't turn Beyoncé and Usher songs into bass-drum-guitar workouts. And the dance moves they copied from the videos? Beyond lame.

Even Mad Unicorn, the supposed riot-girl band of Federal Hill, was disappointing. They played a hit by one of those Simpson sisters—I can't remember which one—even though those Simpson chicks wouldn't know a riot if an entire city was burning at their feet. Mad Unicorn sounded more like four gossip girls on a joy ride to the mall, cranking the radio and singing along.

Don Daddio took the mic. He told the audience there was only one more act but that he himself had heard this new band practicing and they were amazing.

"What's he talking about?" I said. "Has he even heard us once?"

"Just some words of encouragement, I guess," said Jonny.

"This is going to be a disaster."

I took a deep breath, and the four of us squeezed through the crowd toward the stage. Just as I was about to climb the steps, someone grabbed me by the arm.

"Good luck, Annabelle," said my mom, catching her breath. Shaky Jake and X stood just behind her, both smiling.

"Mom! What are you doing here? What about the gig? What about PJ Harvey?"

"Your dad's— Well, we decided he's going to do this one as a solo show. As soon as we got to the theater, I started to think, Who needs me more, my kids or Benny and Joon? So Jake and I took a cab to the train station, and here we are."

"I didn't want to miss it, either," Jake said.

"Is Dad mad?" I said.

"Yup," said Jake.

"Sweetie, don't worry. I'll handle that," my mom said. "We'll work it out. Just go up there and play."

"Okay, Mom." I went in for a hug, swiveling into my mom's left side while X grabbed on to the right. I couldn't believe my mom had shown up, and I really did want to make her proud, but I squirmed away and let X take the bulk of the sugary smooching.

Rock stars' moms do not hug and kiss them before a show.

"Go on now, get up there," Mom said.

"Give 'em hell, guys!" Jake called out.

"Mom," I said, "I don't want to move back to Brooklyn. I want to stay in Providence now. Don't make me leave, okay?"

"Of course, Annabelle," she said, hugging me again, tighter than before. "And I want you right here with me. We're going to make this work."

I kissed my mom on the cheek, then turned and ran up the stairs. Crackers and Jonny had already been checking cords and amp levels for a minute.

"You're all set," Jonny said. "Everything's ready to go."

I looked over at Jake, who gave me the thumbs-up sign. Then I called the band over to a corner of the stage behind the drum set. We formed a circle, and I put my hand out. *This is how Ronaldo would do it,* I thought. It felt cheesy, but it also felt right. Jonny, Crackers, and Darren put their hands on top of mine.

"This is it, guys," I said. "Everything we've been working on for the last two months comes down to the next ten minutes. This is the biggest stage we've ever played. I'm glad you guys are my friends, and I know we can do this. Let's let them know who we are."

"The biggest losers in school?" Jonny said.

"Exactly," Crackers said. "We've got nothing to lose."

"Don't sweat it, Belle," Don whispered to me, putting his hand over the mic so he wouldn't be heard. "Raising Cain is just a good cover band. You, my friend, are a songwriter."

"Thanks, Don," I said as he turned back toward the audience.

"Ladies and gentleman, rockers and metalheads, dorks and dweebs, please give a warm welcome to . . . The Bungles!"

After a smattering of applause, I took my place behind the mic and a spotlight hit me right between the eyes. I could make out Crackers on my right, and Jonny and Darren right behind me, but I couldn't see anybody in the crowd. I started to panic, just like I had when Egg Mountain had opened for Deerhoof. Throat-sewn-shut syndrome again. I looked over and saw Christine holding her hand to her forehead like a visor, trying in vain to shield her eyes from the blinding light. My palms were sweating like crazy.

"Just breathe, Annabelle," someone said from behind me. It was Darren. "Three deep breaths. There you go."

I did what he said. One breath, then two more. I looked

into those brown eyes of his, and they made me relax. Darren calmed me down the way Ronaldo used to. He made me feel like there was nothing but music—music and us.

"So let's tear the roof off this place," Darren said.

"We're outside," I said, looking up. "This place doesn't have a roof."

"True," Darren smiled. "You cool?"

"Yep," I said, turning to look at him. "Thanks, Darren."

"No prob. We're gonna knock 'em dead."

I looked out at the sound guy. "Can you put a little more bass in my monitor? Thanks."

Then I moved back a foot, and the new angle made it easier to see the audience and my bandmates, too. Crackers did the same, and nodded in my direction. All four of us met eyes, and Darren counted off "Is This It."

"One, two," he shouted, clicking his sticks in time. "One, two, three, four."

Crackers and I came in with vocals right away, trading verses, and we were each off-kilter at first—I could barely hear my own voice through the monitors, and Crackers looked a little confused herself—but by the time the first chorus came, we were locked in. A few people in the front started to clap along.

"Sing it, Belle!" I heard Jake yell at the top of his lungs.

By the time we got to the bridge, where Crackers really got to sing out, the whole audience was standing for the first time since the Raising Cain set. Darren was pounding out a clean, clear beat, Jonny was slashing away at the rising chord progression, and Crackers and I sang out confidently. We cruised through the final verse and finished with a bang. The audience clapped enthusiastically. It might not have been the total madness that greeted Jackson and his thug-buddies, but it was respectable.

"Thanks, everybody," I said to the audience. "This is our first gig as a full band, and we're really glad to be playing for you tonight. It's a long story, but it almost didn't happen." The Mohawk sound guy, manning the console way in the back, gave me a thumbs-up. At that moment, he seemed cool, and I thought, *We can still win this.* But Jackson stood just in front of the soundboard, preening.

I brought out the new-and-improved lyrics I had scrawled on paper only a few minutes earlier. I had changed the title from "Where Do I Go (From Here)?" to "Not Goin' Anywhere." I might not have ever performed it before, but I considered it the first full-fledged song I'd ever written. I started, as planned, completely alone. I made sure to look up, using a trick my mom had once taught me: look directly at the last row. Those people are far enough away that it's not scary to look right at them, but the fact that you *are* focusing on the audience makes a huge difference. It makes you look strong, passionate, and intense. And that was exactly how I felt, like there was nowhere else in the world that I'd rather be.

It wasn't my choice
To come to this town
It started off ugly
But I'm turning it around
I'm not goin' anywhere

I came here with shorts on
But now I'm wearing sweaters

Some days are bad
But other days are better
I'm not goin' anywhere

After eight bars, Darren kept time quietly on the high hat. After another eight, Jonny came in and Darren switched to the snare drum.

I came here desperate
To take back what I'd lost
But there wasn't a line
I wasn't willing to cross
I wasn't goin' anywhere

The series of verses—that's right, Mr. V, no chorus!—started its build toward a U2-style climax. Crackers played a synth line and we all locked in, building tension as we went.

But now I'm back
And I know what I need
I'm not the best singer
But I'm learning how to lead
I'm not goin' anywhere

But suddenly, I couldn't hear my voice. I couldn't hear the Beatle bass or my own vocals, either. All I could hear was Darren's popping snare. I checked my cord, and it was fine. But when I looked at my amp, the power light was out. There was no electricity onstage! We were still playing, but to the audience it must have looked like I had lost my voice in the middle of the song! I tried not to freak out. I stepped away from the mic that wasn't even working and belted out the last verse with all the power I could muster.

I still don't know
How this story'll end
I might be pushed, might be punched,
Might be picked up by friends
But now at least
I've got some things to defend
And I'm not goin' anywhere

I drew my finger across my throat, giving the band the kill sign, and just like that, the first performance of a song I had written all by myself puttered to a halt, in like a lion and out like a mouse. I looked at the crowd, and people—not just the back row, either!—were looking up at us in complete confusion. A few started giggling, and, worse, others clapped mockingly.

"Nice one, Cabrera!" someone cried out.

"That's why they call 'em The Bungles!" said somebody else, to a chorus of laughter.

Don was making wild gestures to the sound guy, trying to figure out what was up. Mohawk put on an Oscar-worthy performance, flailing about, switching cords around and generally doing everything he could to mask what I now knew—that Jackson had bribed him into sabotaging our performance. (He had the money, after all!) The audience just got louder, talking, laughing, and enjoying the huge joke that The Bungles had become. Don couldn't even use the mic to tell the audience what was going on and that it wasn't *our* fault that everything had gotten busted halfway into our set. I made eye contact with him, and all he could do was give me a helpless look.

I tapped on a distortion pedal nervously with the toe of my yellow Chuck, and an embarrassing squawk of feedback burst out. Gliding my hand along the neck of the Beatle bass, I suddenly wished I had Satomi. And for a second, I wished I were on Central Park SummerStage being cheered by thousands, rather than booed by a bunch of tweenage goons in Nowheresville, Rhode Island. But as I looked up and gazed out powerlessly at the sea of people in front of me, I saw a face I recognized—a face that I instantly realized could turn The Bungles into the band to beat again. I knew exactly what to do. I put my bass down and headed into the crowd.

"Belle, where do you think you're going?" Jonny asked. "What is going on *now*!?"

"Hey, Angelo!" I called out, plunging into the audience. I had to fight my way to the middle of the crowd, and it took a lot of pushing and shoving, a lot of *sorry*s and *excuse me*s to make it to the boy with the bumblebee shoes.

"Hey, Annabelle," he said, and I whispered in his ear. At first, he looked totally mystified, but as I went on he started to nod slowly. By the time I left him and started fighting my way back to the stage, he was sporting a sneaky smile.

"Tell all your friends," I said.

Angelo turned to a couple of friends and whispered the news to them. Soon he was moving through the crowd, and so were his friends, each finding someone new to share the secret with.

By the time I got back to the stage, a big chunk of the audience—maybe twenty or twenty-five kids—was whispering to each other. It was like a massive game of telephone. I looked out and I could actually see a wave of turning heads. A kid would get the message, turn to pass it on to whoever was standing on the other side of him, and then start walking toward the front of the crowd. They eventually formed a line and snaked their way up to the stage to join us. It was stage invasion by an army of the littlest and most picked-on kids at Federal Hill. They were our reinforcements in the war on Raising Cain.

"What's going on?" Jonny asked.

"Oh, just an idea in the we've-got-nothing-to-lose category, I guess. Hey, help those guys get up here, will ya?"

"Some of these kids aren't exactly my biggest fans," he whispered.

"Well, now's your chance to start making up for it."

Jonny and I both moved to the edge of the stage and reached our hands down to pull up the kids. Others scurried on from the stairs at stage right, where Crackers and Darren greeted them.

Angelo tugged at my sleeve. "I'm into the idea, but I don't know about *him*," he said, pointing to Jonny. "Or *him*," pointing to Darren.

"They're done with that, I promise," I said. Jonny gave him a hesitant wave and kept his distance. Darren just slunk away, staring intently at his drumsticks.

"Hey, Bass Goddess." X jumped on the stage, armed with his clapping monkey and a pair of mini-maracas. "Can I join in?"

"Sure thing, X. Just make a lot of noise, okay?"

"Done."

"Okay, all you guys, gather over here." I directed the kids to the space between the drum kit and the back of the stage and started singing the chorus to "A Place in the Sun." "So Christine here is going to sing all the verses, okay? She's the only one with a voice big enough to sing on her own. But when we get to the chorus, I want you guys to sing out as loud as you can. Sing it right to you-know-who, okay?" They nodded.

I walked to the front of the stage and started waving my hands, trying to get the audience's attention. The crowd was still murmuring, so I had to really yell to be heard.

"Well, as you can see, we're having some technical difficulties, but we've been practicing too long and hard to quit now," I said. "So we're going to try a little sing-along and see how it goes."

Jonny pulled out his acoustic guitar and Darren got ready on the drum set—these were the only two instruments that didn't rely on power at all—and started playing the opening chords to the song. I motioned to the kids to clap along with me on beats two and four, and Crackers started in on the first verse as loudly as she could.

She sang it with more feeling than ever before, and when the crowd got a taste of what she could do, they started to quiet down. Her clear, urgent voice rang through the air, and it worked its effect on the audience. I looked around at the motley crew of bullied kids in front of her and made sure they were ready to sing the chorus. Twenty-five eager nods. All set.

Those Stevie Wonder lyrics definitely fit the moment perfectly. They're all about how there's a place under the sun for everyone and how no one should feel left out and how bullies are lame. Stevie said it a little differently, but that's the idea. When the little dudes joined us, their voices easily carried out into the audience. We sounded like more than a band; it was now a full-on rock 'n' roll choir—the acoustic instruments, plus twenty-five children's voices rising up in song. It might not have equaled the honed metallic attack of Raising Cain, but The Bungles had given birth, again, to something new and different.

I looked out at the crowd and saw that most of the audience was now swaying in rhythm and singing along. My mom was smiling from ear to ear. A few people were waving lighters or cell phones in the air. Don Daddio and Shaky Jake had their arms around each other's shoulders, rocking back and forth and joining in with The Bungles Children's Choir.

Suddenly, I got a wave of inspiration. "Darren, Jonny, keep going, okay?" I said, climbing up on one of the monitor speakers. I'm not 100 percent sure of this, but I think Darren winked at me, super quickly. I chose to pretend that he didn't—I refused to have a maybe-crush on a winker.

"We've got a dedication of our own to make," I yelled out. "This one is for our good buddy Jackson Royer, and it's brought to him directly by the kids whose hard-earned cash he's been stealing every day."

Eight or ten kids in the crowd gasped "Oooooh" in unison. Others looked around, still not getting it.

"Yep. Jackson plays a mean guitar and sings for the best band in town, but that doesn't mean he has the right to mess with me and my friends over here." I walked around the stage, looking out across the tightly packed audience. "And it doesn't mean he has the right to pull the plug on our performance."

Jonny couldn't stop smiling. He raised his acoustic up in the air and strummed skyward.

The band continued the slow, insistent groove behind me, underscoring each word. Suddenly Don appeared onstage, handing me a second acoustic guitar.

"Hey, Jackson, you're right," I said, strapping it on and strumming the chords along with Jonny. "It's a humbling thing to have friends. That is, when you actually do have some. You should try it sometime."

The audience started making noise, and some started chanting, "Bungles, Bungles!"

"We've had enough of your strutting around, Jackson," I said, to cheers.

"And enough of your lame jokes," Darren yelled.

"And enough of your bad breath," screamed Jonny.

A few audience members walked toward Jackson and his bandmates. Within seconds, Raising Cain was surrounded. I never thought I'd see Jackson look even so much as slightly off his game, but he looked truly intimidated. He was a smart kid, though, and motioned for the rest of the band to follow him out of the lot before things got out of hand.

"I'll be back, Annabelle, you can bet on it," he called out, beating a quick retreat onto the street and disappearing into the night.

"You suck," Jackson's new drummer called out weakly to us.

"Dorks!" yelled the bassist. But Raising Cain's lame parting words were swallowed up by the cheers of the crowd.

I saw Don at the edge of the stage and approached him.

"Do we have time for one more, Don?" I asked. "The one that got cut off?"

"Sure thing," he said.

I motioned to Crackers. "Hey, you think you could sing 'Not Goin' Anywhere'? I'll give you the lyrics."

"Yeah, I think so."

"Good, because you're the only one who can carry it without the PA."

"No problem. I'll belt it out."

"Ready, guys?" I asked Darren and Jonny. They gave silent nods, and the army of kids, realizing their role was over, formed a phalanx behind us.

Darren counted off, and Crackers sang my song better than I ever could have myself. I couldn't have been more pleased. For once I was happy to be the bassist—just the bassist. I had to laugh to myself when she sang, "I'm not the best singer / But I'm learning how to lead." She was one of the best singers I had ever heard, and the audience obviously agreed. They stayed quiet so they could hear every syllable that Crackers uttered. Jonny, Darren, and I huddled toward the back of the stage, playing our acoustic instruments as loudly as we could, building toward a luminous crescendo. As we held the last chord, Crackers belted the last note and added a series of breathtaking trills and gospel-style flourishes.

The audience roared its approval, and I knew we had won. First place or not, we had won the battle of the bands.

Finally, to a chorus of cheers and whistles, we put our instruments down. Crackers, Jonny, and Darren joined me at the edge of the stage, and The Bungles Children's Choir formed a line behind us. The crowd went absolutely bonkers. I looked over at my mom, who was wiping away tears. Don was on her left, Jake on her right. As the last light disappeared from the sky, the four of us linked arms and waved to the audience. They only yelled louder. We bowed three times, and the crowd screamed our name over and over. The chants of "Bungles, Bungles!" bounced across the buildings on Thayer Street and echoed through the night.

ENCORE

My Work of Art (Revised)

by Annabelle Cabrera

Today I listened to a recording of my band playing live at the Minor Threat Battle of the Bands a week ago. (We came in second—because half the audience wound up onstage with us during our best number, our cheers never eclipsed Raising Cain's—but I prefer to think of it as losing the battle, winning the war.) The last song we performed was the same one I had turned in earlier as my "work of art." And it sounded . . . just okay. It's definitely no work of art.

But I realized that's okay.

Who knows if I'll ever write songs as great as Lennon and McCartney's, or be able to compose bass lines as sweet as Satomi Matsuzaki's. I know how to form a band. I know how to lead a band. And my band is my work of art.

Will this band ever take over the world, change people's lives, and land me and my friends on magazine covers and TV shows, giving interviews that are translated into dozens of different languages? I've got no idea. But I do know that I've found the one thing in my life that I will never stop doing, no matter what. My family could disintegrate, I could find myself halfway around the world in a new city, I could lose all my friends. But wherever I land, I'll find my band.

Despite the fact that The Bungles didn't win the battle—apparently, the fact that we had all the kids join us onstage disqualified us—it was an absolutely perfect night, maybe even better than when I played to twenty times as many people in Central Park. I didn't stop smiling for three days afterward, and it took me a while to count all the reasons why. What I finally realized was that the battle was the new greatest night of my life because I had had to work so hard to make it happen. I will always treasure my Egg Mountain days, of course—EM is great, Ronaldo is one of my best friends, and the Mountain gave me my first experience of being in a band. But it was pure luck stepping into those shoes. With The Bungles, on the other hand, I had to fight and sweat the whole way for absolutely everything we achieved (and we haven't really achieved *anything* yet!). As Shaky Jake would say, I had to "make my own luck," and I think that's why it felt so good.

Here's something else that felt good: the demise of Jackson Royer. It turns out the daughter of Federal Hill's vice principal is in Mad Unicorn, so she was at the battle and saw the whole thing go down. It wasn't hard for her to put two and two together and identify Jackson as the head of the lunch money crime ring. When we got back to school the Monday after the battle, Jackson was nowhere to be found. The rumor mill said he'd been kicked out of school for good, but a week later he was back, having served a one-week suspension.

I could see right away that Jackson wasn't the same guy. Now he walks all hunched over and won't look anybody in the eye. Even his hair has changed; instead of the gooped-up slickie that was his trademark, his hair is flat and unwashed, his bangs hanging in front of his eyes. The proud rooster from just days earlier has been replaced by a sad, whipped dog. He would never bother any of the littlest kids at Federal Hill again, or hassle Jonny or Darren, either. He just sticks to himself now, looking like he can't wait for eighth-grade graduation—that is, if he's lucky enough to see it.

Jonny and Darren, on the other hand, have started walking through the halls with a confidence they're slowly earning, not from bullying but from the respect and trust of the other kids. They've decided to pay back every cent to every kid, even if it takes them a year of raking leaves, shoveling snow, mowing lawns, and whatever other small jobs they can get around Providence. After watching them work their butts off three weekends in a row, I took pity on them and suggested an idea: why not record a quick-and-dirty EP, sell it, and give the profits back to the kids. Whatever money is left over, we agreed, we'd put in a recording fund for our first *real* album, which I'm already starting to write songs for. We're going into the "studio," i.e., my living room, next week.

I'm not sure what's going on with my parents. My dad still wants to tour next summer, after the new Benny and Joon record comes out. My mom wants to spend the summer with us and maybe, for once, take us on an actual vacation. They are being nicer to each other, but something's up. Once a week, they walk up to College Hill "to talk to someone." I think this means that they sit in a room on opposite sides of a couch while a therapist tells them how to fix things. So far, it's not exactly working, but it's not *not* working, either. The thing is, I'm not really sure what I want to happen. X and I get to spend more time with Mom now, which is excellent. But whenever Dad enters the room, I can feel the tension between them. It's like it takes so much energy for them to be nice to each other that they forget, again, that X and I are right there next to them. Jake says to just wait it out, so that's what I'm going to do.

Abuela calls me twice a week now, once on Sunday after she gets back from church and once on Thursday so she can tell me what happened on the *Real Housewives* show that her cousin Juanita has gotten her addicted to. She tells me all the crazy things that Juanita says and does, and all the church gossip. Then she asks if there are any boys I like at school, even though in her world you don't ever date. You just get married young and have tons of babies (which is *definitely* not going to happen to me!). I tell her that there is this one boy with curly hair and brown eyes, but he doesn't know I exist. The truth is, of course, Darren does know I exist, but he doesn't know I have a crush on him (I don't think). It's way too early to mess things up with The Bungles by intro- ducing a John and Yoko/Dean and Britta/Kim and Thurston angle to the group, and to be honest, it's way too early for me to be dealing with that at all. I've got homework to do, songs to write, and a band to manage, after all. It's more than enough for a twelve-year-old girl to handle.

X has been really happy and surprisingly mellow for the past few days. Why? Because Abuela has agreed to come to Providence for Christmas, only two weeks away! And even better, Ronaldo's going to come up for New Year's! R says he's coming up here just because Abuela is. They're a package deal, he says. He claims he just wants to have some of her home-cooked food over the holidays, although I think he might also be interested in catching up with a friend and possibly stealing some secrets from the hottest new band in New England.

I'm trying to picture us having our holidays in what is, after all, just a recording studio with a kitchen and a couple of Japanese screens. X will be overjoyed, I'm sure; he's still at the age where he wakes up at five a.m. on Christmas morning, totally unable to sleep. Abuela will give him a Hallmark card with some incredibly gushy grandma stuff written in unreadable script, plus the same crinkly ten-dollar bill she includes in it every year. And again, like every year, it'll be his favorite present by a mile.

When Ronaldo arrives, he'll probably play me about a million new songs on his iPod, but we'll wind up talking about The Beatles, The Kinks, and Deerhoof, just like we always do.

And we'll talk about the Rules to Rock By, and how much more of a master I am than he is. Ha! (Not really.) I wonder whether Shaky Jake will stay with us this year. If he does, he'll know to stay well clear of the kitchen, because that was, is, and always will be Abuela's domain, even if she's never visited the Rhode Island apartment before.

How will my parents be getting along two weeks from now? It's hard to say. Maybe they'll pull through the way they always have before and be happier than ever. Or maybe they'll split up and my dad will go on tour for the next eight years. That would be horrible, but how can you know what adults are going to do? They're even crazier and harder to figure out than kids. But as I imagine this Christmas, surrounded by Ronaldo, Jake, Abuela, and hopefully Darren, Crackers, and Jonny, too, I'm not worried about the future. I've got my friends, I've got my family, and I've got my band. And for now, that's good enough. Better than good enough.

Plus, yesterday, Darren called me on the phone. I asked him if I'd forgotten about a scheduled practice, and he laughed and said, no, he just wanted to talk.

"Why?" I asked.

"Um, because we're friends, I guess," he said. "Because I think you're awesome."

Okay, so maybe rock stars do *blush. Sometimes.*

ACKNOWLEDGMENTS

I want to thank the many friends who supported and encouraged me as I wrote this book: Linden and Carl Berry, Mac Hanger, Dennis and Vicki Farrar, Tayef Ben Messalem, Aimee Molloy, Chris Daddio, Shelby Gaines, Sue Mason, Michel Galante, Kevin March, Seth Unger, Karla Schickele and the Willie Mae Rock Camp for Girls, Marlene Clary and everyone at Creative Arts Program, Laura Rozos, Lisa Dwyer, Dan Efram, Serena Kuo, Jacob Bricca, Naomi Hamby, Tim Walker, Fred Wasch, Justine Skyers, Nova Perry, Kiran Kapur, Kirsten Gustafson-Kapur, Sofie Kapur and the awesome Blame The Patient, Jen London, Marc and Audrey Engelsgjerd, Mark Ryan, Jennifer Schwartz, Megan McGuinness, Irene Borland, Sarah O'Holla, Sarv Taghavin, Andie Levinger, Irwin Walkenfeld, Kathleen Admirand-Dimmler, Laura Quinlan Hug, Karencia Ible, Rebecca Zelo, Gabby Danchick, Susanna Einstein, Michael Milone, James Luria, Amy Ellenbogen, Patrick McNulty, Julie Mazur Tribe, Lise Clavel, my amazing agent, Marissa Walsh, and my fantastic editor, Stacy Cantor.